Leap of
FAITH

ANNE SCHRAFF

SADDLEBACK
EDUCATIONAL PUBLISHING

URBAN UNDERGROUND

SADDLEBACK
EDUCATIONAL PUBLISHING
www.sdlback.com

© 2011 by Saddleback Educational Publishing

ISBN-13: 978-1-61651-588-1
ISBN-10: 1-61651-588-0
eBook: 978-1-61247-234-8

Printed in Guangzhou, China
0411/04-56-11

16 15 14 13 12   1 2 3 4 5

CHAPTER ONE

Ernesto Sandoval had been thinking of running for senior class president at Cesar Chavez High School. Kids were running for vice president and treasurer too. But the senior president election was what most students followed.

Ernesto had been turning the idea over in his mind for weeks. Sixteen-year-old Ernesto had been a student there for just his junior year. He had been born here in the *barrio*. But his father got a job teaching in Los Angeles, and the family had lived there for ten years. Then Luis Sandoval got a job teaching history at Chavez, and the family returned to its roots.

Ernesto had made a lot of friends at Chavez. The tall, handsome young man was well liked and friendly. But he'd be running against Mira Nuñez, a popular, beautiful junior. She had lived here all her life and started Chavez as a freshman. She was already junior class vice president. Also running was Rod Garcia. He'd been president of several clubs on campus. Ernesto knew it wouldn't be easy to convince students to choose a newcomer like him.

"I really think I could do a good job as a senior class president," Ernesto told his girlfriend, Naomi Martinez.

"Then go for it, Ernie," Naomi urged him. "A lot of kids like and respect you. You've been here only a short time. But you've had a big impact on a lot of lives. Take what you and your dad do, for example. You walk around the *barrio* getting dropouts to come back to school. I can't believe the good you've done in such a short time. People notice that, Ernie."

2

Ernesto smiled at the beautiful, violet-eyed girl. Her dark, curly hair framed her lovely face. "Of course, that's an unbiased opinion coming from the girl I love," Ernesto replied with a wry grin.

"The girl who loves you, Ernie," Naomi told him. "But honest, I'm not just saying this because I love you. You've touched so many kids in a good way. You know what I'm talking about. I don't have to go through the list. Poor little Yvette Ozono was a lost soul. Then you and your dad took her under your wings. And Julio Avila, he almost ruined his whole life that day pulling out a knife in a fight. But you and Abel got the switchblade away from him. Dom Reynosa and Carlos Negrete would have left school long ago except for you and your dad. You were part of the *Zapatistas* who help Mr. Ibarra become councilman. You helped get Oriole and Starling streets repaved. Ernesto, you saved me from that madman who tried to abduct me late one night after work. If not for you, I might not be alive today!"

"Well," Ernesto said, "I guess I could file. Couldn't hurt, as *Abuela* always says."

Ernesto's best friend, Abel Ruiz, was walking toward them. When Ernesto had first attended Chavez, he was a frightened stranger. Abel was the first to reach out to him, and they became best friends. "Hey Ernie," Abel hailed.

"Hey Abel, Naomi thinks I should file for senior class president," Ernesto said. "She thinks I got a chance."

"More than a chance," Naomi declared. "You've changed lives."

"You sure changed *my* life, *amigo*," Abel asserted. "I was so down on myself that I thought I was a hopeless loser. My big brother Tomás was the star in our family. Mom never got tired of telling me I was a loser. Nobody expected anything of me. Then you talked to me, Ernie. You came on strong. You said I needed to go for my dream. I was ashamed to even tell anybody that I *had* a dream. But you got it out of me."

Abel nodded and pointed at his friend. "*You* were the first person I ever told how much I loved cooking—that I wanted to be a chef. Now I'm studying cooking. When I finish at Chavez, I'm goin' to culinary arts school. I'm cookin' meals for my friends and collectin' kudos. I feel like somebody. You gave me the courage to be myself, Ernie."

"See?" Naomi asked, smiling. "You helped Abel realize his dream. You got Carlos and Dom off the street. They were just tagging walls and fences. Then Abel came up with the idea of them painting that beautiful mural on the science building. And you ran with Abel's idea, Ernie. Maybe a third of the kids who go to school here have been blessed to know you."

"Wow!" Ernesto exclaimed. "Now I'm getting excited. I don't think I'll bother running for senior class president. I think I'll run for king of the world."

"Ernie!" Naomi chided with mock anger, punching him lightly in the shoulder.

"Naomi's right," Abel agreed. "You're a great guy, Ernie, and everyone sees that."

Ernesto headed for English class. When he walked into the room, he saw a small stack of filing applications on Ms. Hunt's desk. Ernesto went up and took one. Ms. Hunt was a young woman and probably one of the best teachers at Chavez.

"You thinking of running for senior office, Ernesto?" Ms. Hunt asked him.

"Yeah, I was kicking the idea around," Ernesto replied.

"Good idea," the teacher told him. "There are a lot of wonderful students in the junior class, Ernesto. But they need motivation. Somebody like you could inspire many of them. The dropout rate here at Chavez is pretty bleak. We need all the good leaders we can get."

"Thanks for the vote of confidence, Ms. Hunt," Ernesto responded. He was touched and impressed that the teacher saw him in that way. Ernesto always had the feeling that Ms. Hunt liked him. He did well in class. When a problem arose, she often turned to him to give her a hand. Two weeks ago, a disturbance had occurred outside her classroom. An argument was turning into an ugly confrontation between two girls. Ms. Hunt didn't hesitate to turn her class over to Ernesto while she went outside to break it up. Ernesto kept things going for twenty minutes until she returned.

At midday, Ernesto brought the application with him to fill it out during his lunch period. Usually he ate lunch with Julio Avila, who was on the track team with him. Abel, Dom, and Carlos were typically there too.

"Hey man," Julio asked, "you runnin' for something?"

"Yeah," Ernesto answered. "Senior class president. You're always beating me in the hundred yard dash. Maybe I can win here."

"Oh boy," Dom Reynosa exclaimed. "Me and Carlos'll make campaign posters for you, dude. We're great artists, you know. When we first met you, man, we were tagging a fence. You took one look at the stuff we were doing and said maybe we could be muralists. You know, like those famous Mexican guys."

"Yeah," Carlos told Ernesto. "You turned us around, Ernie. Now we're sticking it out here at Chavez.

"Even though we're bored stiff most of the time," Dom added glumly.

Ernesto completed the application. On his way out of school after the last bell, he dropped it off at the vice principal's office. He knew that Mira Nuñez and Rod Garcia had already filed. But he didn't think any other juniors would. "Well," Ernesto thought, "one chance in three wasn't bad."

Ernesto jogged home from school to his home on Wren Street. When the weather was good, as it was today, he liked to run. Jogging improved his track performance and it was fun. Ernesto always felt better after a run.

Ernesto's father wasn't home when the boy got there. Mr. Sandoval was still at his desk at Cesar Chavez high school. But Maria Sandoval, Ernesto's mother, was home. She'd just brought Ernesto's two little sisters home from elementary school. Eight-year-old Katalina and six-year-old Juanita had run to their *Abuela* Lena, Dad's widowed mother. Grandma had been living with the family for several months now. She helped the girls with their homework and played games with them. Ever since *Abuela* Lena had moved in, the girls were less interested in video games and TV.

"Hi Mom," Ernesto called. He had talked to his parents about running for senior class president. "I filed today for senior class president, Mom."

"Good for you!" Mom popped her head through the kitchen doorway, smiling. "I'm so glad. You have natural leadership qualities."

Mom didn't work outside the home. But she had written a published children's picture book a few months ago—*Thunder and Princess*. It was the story of a pit bull and a cat, based on a neighbor's dog, Brutus. When the book was published, Mom made a few appearances at bookstores. Mom was smart. She'd graduated from high school with honors. She'd planned to go to college and become a writer. But then she met Luis Sandoval, and she never made it to college. Mom's parents, especially her mother, were disappointed that their only child's bright future was shut down. Mom's mother often lamented that her daughter had "wasted her gifts." They were very happy when Mom had her book published. Now Mom was having another child. She was working on a second book. But she knew she might have to put it aside for a while after the baby was born.

Ernesto noticed that his mother looked a little downcast, despite her smile. "Everything okay, Mom?" he asked.

"Oh sure. It's just that my mom called me this morning," Maria Sandoval explained. "That's usually something of a downer."

"Want to talk, Mom?" Ernesto asked.

"I guess so," Mom replied. She brought coffee out to the living room for herself and her son. They sat at either side of an end table.

"You know, honey, the baby is due in about three months. Mom sorta got on me for having another baby at this time in my life—*at my age.*"

Ernesto frowned. He really loved *Abuela* Lena, his dad's mom. But he never cared much for Eva Vasquez, his mother's mom. Alfredo Vasquez, Eva's husband, was okay, but Ernesto's grandmother was a bit of a pain.

Eva Vasquez had cherished her daughter as gifted and beautiful. *Abuela* thought her daughter was destined for great things. Perhaps she would be a college professor at an Ivy League university or even a CEO of a large and influential company. Instead, she married a schoolteacher, Luis Sandoval, and settled into the drudgery of being a housewife.

11

"Mom," Ernesto asked, "what's this stuff about 'at your age'? You're still a young woman!" Ernesto thought his grandmother had a lot of nerve berating his mother. The baby was none of *Abuela*'s business. Having another baby was between his parents. Grandma had no say in it. She should be gracious enough to keep her opinions to herself.

"Yeah," Mom agreed. "But she's like saying I was finally done with the girls needing a lot of my time. Now maybe I could go to college and get that degree she always wanted for me. Mom said I had a window of opportunity to achieve my potential at last. Now I was having another baby. Then I'd be stuck with dirty diapers and toilet training. It'd be years and years before the child was even ready for preschool. Mom was saying it was so great that I got that book published. Now, instead of really pursuing my writing career, I'll be taking care of a baby."

"Mom," Ernesto said softly. "It's none of her business, you know."

"Oh, I know that, honey," Mom agreed. "And I'm really happy about the baby. I'm excited, and I've never felt healthier than I do right now. When I think of another little boy, it just thrills me. But my mom has a way of making the best things seem like disasters."

"I wish she'd keep out of our lives," Ernesto remarked. He knew he was being harsh, but that was how he felt.

"Honey, I love my mom," Mrs. Sandoval told her son. "I know you've never been too thrilled with her and I understand that. But she's been a wonderful mother. She just doted on me. I know she loves me very much, and she loves you guys too. When the baby comes, she'll love him too."

His mother sighed and sipped her coffee. "But right now, well, she and Dad are coming down for dinner on Sunday— and I dread it. Dad, of course, is fine with the baby. He's excited about us naming the baby after him. He was always a little disappointed that we didn't name you

Alfredo. But now Dad is going to have a grandson named after him. So he's fine. But Mom . . ." Ernesto's mother sighed again, this time more deeply.

"Just ignore what she says, Mom. Just let her talk," Ernesto advised.

"Oh honey!" Mom chuckled, smiling ruefully. "Here I am dumping my troubles on you. My wonderful sixteen-year-old son brought home wonderful news. He's going to run for senior class president and make us all proud. And I'm a big wet blanket."

Mom reached over and caressed her son's face. "I'm sorry, Ernie. But, you know, I can't talk to your father about this. I can't cry on his shoulder. Because then he gets the guilts. By marrying him, I shut off my bright future as who knows what? At least, that's how he feels. But I have no regrets at all. When I look at your dad and you guys, I feel like the luckiest woman on the face of the earth. But Mom thinks I should be teaching classical studies at Harvard or leading some high-tech company into the green revolution. She thinks my picture should be on the front page of the *Wall Street Journal*!"

"Can't you keep her at bay with that new book you're writing, Mom?" Ernesto suggested. Maria Sandoval was working on a new picture book about a baby panda. The panda was born at the local zoo. Then she got to the age when she had to return to China and a whole new world. Mom was well along in the book, and her agent liked it a lot. "I'll try," Mom sighed, "I'll show her the rough draft."

Ernesto heard his sisters and *Abuela* Lena laughing in the front room. They were just playing a game. Sometimes *Abuela* let them win just to build up their self-esteem. She was like that.

"Who else is running for senior class president, Ernie?" Mom asked.

"Rod Garcia," Ernesto responded, happy to be off the subject of *Abuela* Eva. "He's president of the Ecology Club and the Science Club. He's a nice guy, but not

15

very outgoing. My real competition is going to come from Mira Nuñez. She's pretty and popular. She's junior vice president now, and that's gonna help her. She's run for office before and won. This is my first shot."

"Isn't she Clay Aguirre's girlfriend?" Mom asked.

When the Sandoval family first moved back to the *barrio*, Ernesto was a stranger at Chavez. Early on, he spotted a lovely girl, Naomi Martinez. Ernesto was attracted to Naomi immediately, but she was Clay Aguirre's girlfriend. Ernesto was disgusted by the rude way Clay treated his girl. But she stuck with Clay until they had a bad fight and he punched her in the face. Naomi dumped Clay after that. Gradually, Naomi and Ernesto got close. Now they were in love. Clay never accepted losing Naomi. He kept trying to get her back. He started dating Mira Nuñez, trying to make Naomi jealous enough to return to him. But she didn't and never would.

"Mira and Clay are going together, Mom," Ernesto replied. "A few weeks ago, they came into Chill Out, that yogurt place where Naomi works. Naomi heard Clay treating Mira the same way he used to treat Naomi. He was mad that Mira hadn't finished a school paper for him. He was all like yelling at her and calling her stupid and a dummy. Naomi said she couldn't believe a beautiful, smart girl like Mira was taking that from the creep. But then Naomi remembered she was the same way. She put up with so much from Clay because he can be charming and nice. Then something annoys him and he goes off."

"You know, Ernie," Mom commented, "I've often thought Naomi put up with Clay's rudeness for so long because that's how she grew up in that home. Her dad is sometimes disrespectful to his wife. Felix Martinez is nicer now. But I've been there when he's called his wife some very ugly names. I think Naomi thought that's the

17

way guys treat girls and women. She thought that's normal behavior."

"Yeah," Ernesto agreed. "I think you're right, Mom. Of course, Clay's gonna go all out to try to get Mira elected. For one thing, he hates me for taking Naomi away from him. It would burn him up if I got the senior class president spot. I don't think he even cares that much for Mira. He just wants to spite me."

Luis Sandoval, Ernesto's father came through the doorway at that moment. He was one of the few teachers at Cesar Chavez High School who didn't leave right after classes ended. He always sat at his desk for at least thirty minutes. Perhaps a student wanted to talk to him about the class or even about personal problems. Ernesto thought that was pretty cool of Dad.

Mom took the coffee mugs into the kitchen. Dad dropped his briefcase by the door and went in to kiss her hello.

Ernesto loved his father and respected him deeply. He was a guy who cared not only for his family, but also for his students and for the whole *barrio*.

Luis Sandoval often walked the mean streets of the *barrio*. He struck up conversations with aimless kids who had dropped out of school. He would dig for something that they were interested in. Then he would use that to lure them back. He played one-on-one basketball with some of them. He did anything he could to get close enough to them to pull them back into school. He wasn't always successful, but he had his success stories. He had already lured half a dozen dropouts back into classes at Chavez.

Mr. Sandoval emerged from the kitchen. "So, is it true, Ernie?" Dad asked.

"Yeah, Dad," Ernesto affirmed. "How'd you know?"

"Ernie, I ran into Abel Ruiz today," Dad explained. "He said you were about to file. He thought it was a great idea, and it is. You know, Ernie, you've been talking about maybe getting a law degree and even going into politics. This would be a great introduction to the process of running for an office. When you helped get Emilio Ibarra elected to the city council, I was really proud of you. I guess that gave you a taste of the process, and you liked it."

Ernesto had joined the group of students dubbed the *Zapatistas*. The group had worked hard for the election of Emilio Zapata Ibarra to the city council. Ibarra was the father of Ernesto's good friend at school, Carmen Ibarra. He was a good, honest man. In office for only months, he had already done some fine things. He helped the homeless veterans who had been living in the ravine. He restored a scholarship program for needy students to go to college. And he acted quickly to get Oriole and Starling streets repaved because they were hazardous to drive on.

Ernesto was proud of his role in helping elect Mr. Ibarra to the city council. Now he was excited about running for a school office for the first time in his life. In Los

Angeles, the most he had ever done was to be the home room monitor.

Ernesto Sandoval had felt strange and lonely when he first arrived at Cesar Chavez High School. Coming into a new school in the eleventh grade was tough. But quickly he had grown to like the students and to love the school. He wanted to do something now for the kids and for the school.

CHAPTER TWO

Emilio Ibarra had defeated Felix Martinez's cousin, Monte Esposito, for the city council seat. Esposito had been the councilman for years but had no longer been serving the people. Shortly after losing the election, the grand jury indicted Esposito for bribery. Naomi's father was bitter about the indictment. He felt that his cousin was innocent and that Ibarra had influenced the grand jury to bring false charges. Martinez hated Emilio Ibarra, and he blamed him for ruining his cousin's life.

Later that afternoon, Ernesto dropped by the Martinez home on Bluebird Street. As soon as Naomi opened the door, he felt gloom in the house. "Let's go in the backyard, Ernie," Naomi suggested. "Dad's in an awful mood."

They went into the backyard of the Martinez home. In the yard, cute little plaster elves presided over a whimsical little rock garden and small pool. Felix Martinez had created the charming little hideaway. Ernesto was always amazed that a man as harsh and often angry as Mr. Martinez could be so creative. But Naomi assured Ernesto that her father had built it all.

Naomi and Ernesto sat on a quaint old bench that Mr. Martinez had also built. Naomi began to talk. "You know, Ernie, Dad's been hoping his cousin would beat those bribery charges. Dad was sure his cousin was clean. You know how Dad loves Monte. When Monte was on the city council, he was always doing nice things for Dad. He even got a picture of Dad with the president of the United States a few years ago. Dad really treasures that photo. Well, Monte just called."

"Uh-oh!" Ernesto groaned. "Don't tell me."

"The worst, Ernie," Naomi explained. "Monte's pled guilty to two of the bribery charges against him. They dropped the four more serious charges for his guilty plea. Monte has to go to jail for six months. But it could have been ten years if he'd been convicted on all the charges."

Naomi looked distressed. "It was such a blow to Dad," she went on, "to hear from Monte's own lips that the bribery charges were true. Dad was always so sure his cousin had done nothing wrong. Dad always said Monte was framed in some big conspiracy led by Emilio Ibarra. Now Monte told Dad he did take expensive gifts in exchange for his votes on the city council. Dad's devastated. He's like a little boy who adored a baseball player. Now he finds out his hero threw the game."

"Oh man!" Ernesto exclaimed. Of course, he always believed Monte Esposito was guilty. But he'd never said so to

Mr. Martinez. Ernesto loved Naomi deeply. He took great pains to keep her father on his side.

For a long time, Ernesto and Felix Martinez had a rocky, almost hostile relationship. Then Ernesto supported Mr. Ibarra for the city council race against Monte Esposito. After that, Naomi's father almost hated Ernesto.

Then, a few weeks ago, a terrible incident at Chill Out changed all that. An armed and crazed man tried to kidnap Naomi. He believed she was his long lost young wife. Ernesto overpowered the armed man, wrested the gun from him, and probably saved Naomi's life. Felix Martinez had hugged Ernesto in gratitude. He called him his fourth son. Ernesto didn't want anything to damage that newfound relationship.

"Where's your father now?" Ernesto asked Naomi.

"He's sitting in the kitchen," she replied. "He's just sitting there. Mom brought him some nice muffins that she'd just made. He growled at her. Oh Ernie, Monte's been Dad's close relative and friend since they were kids. Monte invited Dad to all the big shot dinners when he was a councilman. Dad's so brokenhearted that Monte turned out to be a crook after all."

Ernesto wasn't sure what to do. He didn't want to harm his fragile relationship with Felix Martinez. But he thought he might be able to help. "I'm gonna talk to him, Naomi," Ernesto suggested, "if that's okay with you."

"If you think it'll help, sure, Ernie. But I gotta warn you, he's really raw," Naomi cautioned.

Ernesto went inside the house and walked to the kitchen. When entered the room, Felix Martinez looked up at him. "Come to say 'I told you so,' huh, Ernie? Come to gloat? You worked so hard to get Ibarra in. Then Monte gets hit with those bribery charges."

Mr. Martinez looked away and shook his head. "I had it all figured out. Monte was innocent. That rat Ibarra wasn't satisfied with taking his council seat away. He wanted Monte in jail. I figured it was a bum rap. They were driving a good man down into the ground. But you knew, eh Ernie? You knew all along my cousin was nothin' but a lousy crook. You gotta be laughin' on the inside, Ernie. I guess you got the right. I put my faith in a dirty, rotten—"

As Naomi's father spoke, Ernesto sat down at the kitchen table opposite him. "Monte Esposito isn't a dirty, rotten anything," Ernesto told Mr. Martinez. "He's probably a good man who made some mistakes. When he was on the city council, he probably did a lot of good things. Then he got in trouble. But that doesn't erase the good that he did. A man isn't just the sum total of his mistakes, Mr. Martinez."

Felix Martinez stared at Ernesto. He didn't say a word. He seemed to be in shock.

"Everybody's human," Ernesto went on. "You know, guys get into the system. They see other guys pulling fast ones, and it doesn't seem so bad. Probably your cousin saw stuff going on when he got there. He figured that's how the system works. But that doesn't mean Monte Esposito didn't accomplish some good things in his time."

Mr. Martinez spoke in a soft voice. "Sometimes guys were out of work. Monte got them jobs with the city. Lotta guys with families to support. He took care of them, Ernie. Was a family in the *barrio*. Six kids. And one of the kids had heart trouble. Monte got the Dad work and health insurance, the whole nine yards."

"Well, see?" Ernesto said.

"Yeah," Felix Martinez responded, leaning forward. "But Ernie, none of that counts no more. He's goin' to prison. He's goin' for six months. Monte always got treated with respect. Now he's gonna be in prison with scum. He won't be nothin' no more." The man's voice was distraught.

Ernesto leaned forward too. "Mr. Martinez," he asked, "do you remember some time ago this famous lady? She had a TV show and a magazine and all that? She was busted on a securities rap and sent to prison. She did her time, and everybody said she was finished, but she came back bigger than ever. People didn't respect her less. In fact, they respected her more. They thought, 'Look what she's come through. She did it with grace and dignity.' Now she's bigger and better, Mr. Martinez."

Mr. Martinez turned his head to one side, thinking hard. Ernesto continued. "You tell your cousin to make friends at the prison. Tell him to try to help out the guys there. That's what this lady did. She reached out to the people in prison and helped them. And she came through just fine."

Mr. Martinez nodded slowly. "Yeah, Monte always had a way with people. You're right, Ernie. This doesn't have to break the guy. Monte's strong. He can do this and come out okay on the other side."

"Sure," Ernesto affirmed. "And when he gets out, he can find a place where he can do some good and be happy. His family'll still be there. His friends'll be there. You'll be there. Right, Mr. Martinez?"

"Yeah, you bet I will," Felix Martinez asserted. "I ain't never gonna forget Monte. He never forgot me when he was riding high. No sir!" Mr. Martinez's shoulders had been slumping, but now he straightened up. "I'm gonna call him back, Ernie. I'm gonna tell him all this you been sayin'. I was just so shocked that he admitted to bribery. I wasn't so nice to him, Ernie. I gotta fix that."

Mr. Martinez's face brightened. "Ernie," he declared, "you made me see it in a whole different way, you know? You're all right, boy." Felix Martinez then yelled to his wife, "Linda, Ernie here's staying for dinner. Right Ernie?"

"Sure," Ernesto answered with a smile. He was always happy to be sitting at a dinner table across from Naomi. "Thanks for inviting me. I love your wife's cooking."

Felix Martinez grabbed his cell phone and called Monte Esposito. He was still home. He didn't have to report to the prison for a while. Mr. Martinez went into the den to talk. Ernesto heard snatches of the conversation.

"You'll be okay, Monte," he was saying. "Lissen, we're all behind you, okay? Six months. Hey, that's nothin'. You'll be out of there almost before you unpack your clothes, Monte. . . . Yeah. And when you get out, we'll have a big party, right? You're down for a little while, Monte, but you ain't out. . . . Hey lissen, you're my cousin. You're family. I ain't ever gonna forget all you done for me . . . Listen, Monte. I was talkin' to someone here. He said something very smart. He said, 'Everybody's human, and we all make mistakes.' Don't mean we're not good people, Monte . . ."

The conversation went on a little longer. But Ernesto just smiled and got on his cell phone. He told his mother he'd be having dinner at the Martinez house.

At dinnertime, Mrs. Martinez served delicious fried chicken and mashed potatoes. She announced she had a special *tres leches* cake for dessert.

"So, you runnin' for senior class president, huh Ernie?" Felix Martinez asked, as he had a second helping of fried chicken.

"Yeah," Ernesto responded. "Course, I came to Chavez in my junior year. So I'm not as well-known as the others who're running. So I got my work cut out for me."

Naomi had another helping of fried chicken too. Ernesto marveled at how much she could eat while remaining so skinny. He thought she must have a great metabolism for burning up calories. "Everybody loves Ernie," Naomi declared. "Maybe he hasn't been there long, but he's really touched a lot of kids."

"Yeah," Felix Martinez said, munching chicken. "I can believe that."

After dinner and dessert, Naomi and Ernesto walked outside. They stood at his Volvo for a few minutes. "Ernie, you worked magic with Dad," Naomi told him. "He seems so much more at peace with what happened to Monte."

"Yeah, well," Ernesto mumbled.

"You have a gift for making things better, Ernie," Naomi said. "You're wonderful."

Ernesto grinned. "Yeah, I gotta remember that Sunday when my grandmother comes to visit. She's on Mom's case about having the new baby. She sorta thought that, with my sisters getting older, Mom could go to college. She should accomplish all those big important things she was supposed to do before she met Dad. I really want to tell the lady off. But that would just make matters worse."

They kissed good-bye, and Ernie left for home.

On the drive home, Ernesto noticed a lot of police action at the corner of

Tremayne and Starling. Four police cruisers were parked in front of the thrift store. A small crowd had gathered to see what was going on. Ernesto recognized Paul Morales and Carmen Ibarra standing there. He slowed to a stop and yelled from the window, "What's going down?"

"The thrift store was held up," Carmen shouted back. "Can you believe that? Somebody low enough to rob the thrift store!"

"Did they get the guy?" Ernesto asked.

"No, it just went down. Cops just pulled up," Paul Morales called back. "Some dude wearing a weird mask. He just run up to the old lady at the counter and stuck a gun in her face. Couldn't have gotten more than fifty bucks. Then he took off running."

"The poor lady got so scared. She could've had a heart attack," Carmen said, anger in her voice.

"Yeah," Ernesto agreed, "then the dude would be a murderer."

Ernesto drove on, shaking his head. A lot of robberies and burglaries had been occurring lately. Quite a few men were out of work and desperate. Teenagers who used to get jobs easily couldn't find work. That sad reality was driving up the number of guys willing to take money at gunpoint. Ernesto couldn't imagine pointing a gun at another human being and demanding money. He could understand guys being desperate enough to snatch items from a store. But using a gun was horrifying.

Ernesto was driving toward Wren Street. Suddenly he noticed a skinny guy running down the street as fast as his legs would carry him. He was rushing away from the direction of Tremayne and Starling. He had been wearing a hoodie, but now it was off. Ernesto could see his shaved head. He remembered somebody in the crowd around the thrift store saying the robber wore a hoodie. Suddenly Ernesto recognized the running man by his tattoo.

It was Cruz Lopez, one of the guys Paul Morales ran around with.

Ernesto turned cold and got the shakes. Cruz seemed to be in an awful hurry. He vanished around a dark corner. Was Cruz trying to get out of the area before the police started a search?

Paul Morales had some strange friends. But he swore they were good guys who worked for a living and who helped their families. Both Cruz Lopez and Beto Ortiz had been in minor trouble with the law. They were always being stopped.

Ernesto trusted Paul Morales. But Paul came from the rough side of the railroad tracks. Still, Ernesto didn't want to jump to any conclusions about Cruz. Maybe it was just a coincidence. Maybe he just happened to be running down the street after the thrift store robbery. Maybe he'd done some shoplifting at the little market on Tremayne. Ernesto had seen him doing that a few times.

Then another thought made Ernesto shudder deeply. Maybe Cruz *did* rob the thrift store. But no way would Ernesto call the police on such circumstantial evidence. It just wasn't in Ernesto to get the guy into trouble without being sure. Ernesto thought Cruz was probably innocent. If the police came roaring up to his house, maybe Cruz would do something desperate. Then whatever happened would be all Ernesto's fault.

Earlier in the week, Paul Morales had told Ernesto that he had caught a kid working at the computer store stealing iPhones. Paul collared the kid and, as manager, fired him on the spot. Ernesto remembered asking Paul whether he'd called the police.

Paul Morales had looked at Ernesto as if he was crazy. "Me? Call the cops? No way, José. If I run across a murderer or a rapist—one of those creeps—then, sure, I'd call the cops. But the kid who ripped off the phones is a pathetic loser. He's just trying to make some dirty money. I took the stuff back, and I kicked his behind outta the store. But that's as far as this mother's son goes. I'm not sticking some poor fool with a rap sheet."

Ernesto didn't share all of Paul's attitudes. But he didn't want to call the police on anybody unless he was sure the guy was guilty. Ernesto remembered something Abel had told him once. When he and Paul worked at the donut shop, the owner accused them both of stealing from her. For a while, Abel thought she would even call the cops on Paul. It turned out the owner's daughter was the thief.

When Ernesto got home, he was still thinking about Cruz Lopez. He called Paul Morales on his cell phone. "Hey man," Ernesto asked. "Heard anything more about who ripped off the thrift store?" Maybe Paul or Carmen knew more now than they did when Ernesto spoke with them last.

"Nah," Paul replied. "Probably some drughead trying to get money for his next fix."

Ernesto wished he knew way to hint that he was worried about Cruz Lopez. How could he say he saw Paul's friend running down the street near the thrift store right after the robbery? But Ernesto couldn't go there without setting Paul off. So Ernesto just remarked, "Carmen said she'd help write my campaign slogans when I run for senior class president at school."

"Yeah, she likes you, dude," Paul told him.

At school the next day, Ernesto was at the vending machine, looking for something to eat. He was hoping for something better than the turkey and cheese sandwich he once had. His gaze scanned the selections, and they all looked awful. He finally settled on some peanut butter crackers. They would have to do. He stuck in his money, and the crackers came out with a noisy plunk. A few were cracked.

"You think you got a snowball's chance in hell of beating Mira for senior class president, Sandoval?" Clay Aguirre snarled. Ernesto hadn't even seen Clay come up behind him.

"Well, we'll leave that to the kids who vote," Ernesto replied, forcing his voice to sound calm. He disliked Clay intensely. Clay was a creep and a bully. How he treated girls was especially offensive to Ernesto. Ernesto recalled the sight of Naomi's swollen, bruised face after Clay punched her. Ever since that happened, Ernesto had a special fantasy. He wanted to corner Clay Aguirre in a dark alley and knock his teeth out.

"Mira has it locked up, Sandoval," Clay taunted. "She's been a great junior vice president, and everybody knows and likes her."

At one time, Clay had been pestering Naomi to be his girlfriend again. But Ernesto had scared him into leaving her alone. Now Clay didn't seem so afraid of Ernesto. Maybe Clay felt more confident because he thought Ernesto was going to lose the election badly. Or maybe Clay was just trash-talking because he was scared and nervous. "You're just some jerk who popped in here a few months ago," Clay snarled. Hardly anybody knows you. You come down from Los Angeles acting like a big shot. Well, you're a jerk. And it's almost a joke that you're even running."

"If I haven't got a chance," Ernesto demanded, "why are you getting so worked up, Aguirre? You scared maybe? Go dunk your head in the birdbath! Maybe that'll lower your blood pressure, man."

"You think you're really cool, don't you, Sandoval?" Clay snarled. "You got a big fat ego, and it's built on nothin'. You're a nobody. Mira is gonna get eighty-five percent of the vote. That nerd Garcia will get maybe ten percent from the other geeks. You'll be lucky to get five percent."

"You have a real nice day, Aguirre," Ernesto told him, blowing him off. "I think I see some seagulls circling overhead. If there's any justice in the world, they might

41

relieve themselves on your thick head."
Ernesto turned and walked away.

Ernesto could feel Clay Aguirre's
hateful gaze. It followed him like a laser
beam. Aguirre would never forgive Ernesto
for being with Naomi Martinez. As ugly as
Clay was to the girl, he bitterly resented
losing her.

CHAPTER THREE

At lunchtime that day, Ernesto headed where he usually had lunch with his friends. It was in the shade of some eucalyptus trees. When Ernesto started unwrapping his now crumbled peanut butter crackers, Abel stared at him. "You gotta be kidding, dude," Abel remarked. *"That's lunch?"*

"What?" Ernesto responded. As he unwrapped the paper, his lap filled with crumbs. The peanut butter on the crackers looked gray. "Uh-oh," Ernesto commented sadly, "that vending machine did me in again."

"You want one of my bananas, man?" Julio Avila offered.

"Ernie," Abel said, "my mom used to pack these horrible sandwiches for me to take to school. Now I make my own gourmet sandwiches. I have an extra sandwich right here in my bag. Take it."

Ernesto looked at the sandwich in the Ziploc bag. "You sure you don't want it, Abel?" he asked.

"No, Ernie, I got two for myself," Abel replied.

Dom Reynosa was laughing hard. "The other day, Ernie went over to where the chicks were eating lunch. He was so pathetic, he bummed lunch offa them. Carmen gave him half a sandwich, and the others gave him an apple and a brownie. What's with you, dude? You can tell us. Your family come on hard times or what?"

"No," Ernesto responded. "I just forgot to take something from the fridge. Mom makes wonderful ham and Swiss cheese sandwiches with pickle relish and everything. She even writes our names on the brown bags—Katalina, Juanita, and me."

Dom and Carlos were rolling in the grass laughing. "This guy is like in fourth grade," Carlos roared. "His mommy writes his name on his brown bag. Ernie, you're a lovable fool."

"And these are my friends!" Ernesto remarked, slowly unwrapping the sandwich Abel gave him. "What's in this? It looks good."

"Canadian bacon and spinach and Swiss cheese," Abel answered. "There's a little packet there with ranch dressing that you add just before you eat. Add it too soon, and it makes the bread soggy."

"Abel, maybe you better do it for him," Dom suggested, going into another laughing fit.

"Oh my gosh!" Ernesto exclaimed. "It's even French bread!" He added the dressing and began eating. "Man, this is so good! Boy Abel, thanks a lot!"

Carlos Negrete looked at Dom Reynosa and suggested, "Hey man, let's us forget our lunches tomorrow. Abel, keep that in mind. Tomorrow we're gonna be forgetting our lunches."

When Ernesto was finished eating, he dropped the peanut butter crackers into the trash. It wasn't time yet for afternoon classes to begin. So he asked Dom and the others, "Did you guys hear about the thrift store on Tremayne getting robbed yesterday? I was driving by right after it happened."

"Yeah," Dom replied, "I heard about it. Some jerk got a few bucks. He scared the poor old lady at the counter half out of her wits. What a bummer. What a lame-o."

"I see a lot of guys standing around looking for trouble," Carlos added. "You don't even want to make eye contact with them. Some of them got shaved heads. They wear baggy clothes so they can hide the stuff they steal."

Ernesto took a deep breath. "You guys know Cruz Lopez and Beto Ortiz?" he asked.

"Yeah," Carlos answered. "I don't know them personally. They hang out with

Carmen's boyfriend, Paul. Carmen doesn't like them much. Why do you ask, Ernie?"

"I don't know," Ernesto said. "I've seen them around. Paul says they're okay."

"That Paul Morales is a pretty tough customer," Dom Reynosa remarked. "It surprises me that Carmen's father lets her hang with him. I've seen Cruz grabbing stuff at the twenty-four-seven store and forgetting to pay for it."

"Yeah," Carlos added. "Him and Beto do that all the time."

Abel didn't say anything then. But when he and Ernesto were alone, walking toward class, Abel spoke up. "Cruz's family is really up against it, man. The father lost his job, and they got five in the family. The mom is sick, and they don't have health insurance. So she can't even see a doctor. I seen Cruz ripping off those little tuna fish and crackers. I know that's stealing, but their backs are to the wall."

"Can't they get help from the welfare people or something?" Ernesto asked.

Abel shrugged. "That's a lot of red tape. If you're a single mom with kids, it's a lot easier. But when a dad is in the home, it's tougher to get help."

"Is there anything we can do?" Ernesto asked.

"Well, me and Paul sometimes go grocery shopping for them and take the stuff over. They live in an apartment on Starling," Abel replied.

"I could chip in too," Ernesto offered. "I'm getting pretty good money at the pizzeria. I could do something."

"Paul's gonna pick me up after school," Abel responded. "We were figuring to go to the supermarket and get some stuff. It would be great if you came along. The three of us could fit in Paul's pickup."

"Think we could do it so I can make work at the pizzeria tonight?" Ernesto asked.

"Plenty of time, dude," Abel assured him. "You'll make work on time."

"Hey Abel, you shoulda told me before about this," Ernesto said. "What good are we if we don't help out guys in trouble?"

When Paul pulled up in his truck, he seemed surprised to see Ernesto. "What're you doing here, dude?" he asked.

"Abel told me about how you guys buy groceries for the Lopez family. I'd like to come along and help," Ernesto explained. "I got some cash on me."

"Cool," Paul Morales said.

When the truck was in motion, Ernesto spoke. "Abel told me Cruz's family is so hard up he rips off tuna fish and crackers for them. People shouldn't have to steal to be fed."

"You do what you have to do," Paul commented.

"Five in the family, huh?" Ernesto asked.

"Yeah," Paul responded. "The mom lays around most of the day. She's been to doctors, but they couldn't figure out what was wrong. They told her to come back, but she's got no money. When the dad lost his construction job, that was the end of his health insurance too. Cruz earns chump change, and the other kids are young—nine, ten."

They pulled into the parking lot of the supermarket, and the three boys headed in. They figured out how much they had to spend. Paul kicked in forty dollars, and Abel and Ernesto added thirty dollars each. They went down the aisles of the store with their cart. They loaded it with milk, bread, cheese, ice cream, veggies, spaghetti, ground beef, tuna fish, beans, and nutrition bars. "Look," Abel pointed. "The chocolate chip cookies are on sale."

"Toss in a couple boxes," Paul said.

When they got to the cash register, the bill came to ninety-eight dollars and some cents. The boys loaded it all into the bed of the pickup and headed for Starling Street.

A thin, worried-looking man let the trio into the apartment. He kept mumbling "*Gracias, gracias*" over and over. The boys put the perishables into the refrigerator and freezer and the other food into the cupboard. When Ernesto opened the fridge, he saw a half empty milk container and a yogurt. That was all. After adding the milk, ice cream, more yogurt, butter, and cheese, the refrigerator looked pretty full. The cupboards were pretty bare too. But now there were a lot of cans and boxes of crackers, pasta, rice, beans, and cookies.

The father seemed overwhelmed. "*Gracias*," he said again, almost tearfully.

"*Por nada*," Paul responded. Then Paul spoke with Mr. Lopez in Spanish. He asked where Cruz was. Mr. Lopez said he had not seen his son in several days. He told Paul the boy was getting harder and harder to control. The father was worried about him. Ernesto knew Spanish pretty well, and what Mr. Lopez said worried him. Cruz was out there running wild. Maybe he *was* the one who robbed the thrift store.

The three boys said their good-byes and walked back to the pickup. Ernesto decided he had to say something. "Paul, you know that thrift store robbery on Tremayne?"

"Yeah, what about it?" Paul replied.

"Right after it happened," Ernesto explained, "I saw this guy running down the street. He looked like he might have been coming from the thrift store. He was going really fast, like the devil was after him. It was Cruz."

"Wait a minute!" Paul answered sharply. "Waddya sayin', man? You sayin' you think Cruz mighta robbed the thrift store? Is that what you're sayin' Ernie? Because that's a lotta garbage. Cruz would never pull a piece on some old lady and rip off a thrift store. He's a decent kid."

"Paul, I'm not saying anything," Ernesto explained. "I'm just telling you what I saw."

"Listen up, Ernie," Paul said, glancing over at Ernesto as he drove. "Cruz wouldn't do something like that. I know his heart. I know this kid. He saved my life when I was bitten by a rattlesnake out in Anza-Borrego.

If he hadn't gotten me to the paramedics, I mighta died."

Paul had to look for traffic as he made a turn. He paused, then spoke again. "This is a good kid. He's like my own blood. You saw him running down the street. Maybe he just ripped off some stuff from the fruit stand, and the guy saw him.

Paul was quiet for a second, thinking. "Ernie," he asked, "you didn't say anything to the cops or anything, did you?" Paul's voice was thick with anguish.

"Paul, you know me better than that," Ernesto said.

"Okay, man," Paul sighed, taking a deep breath. "Don't tell anybody. You either, Abel. The cops are always hassling Cruz and Beto. The cops can't get wind of him running away from the thrift store like he was. They'd just find him and bust him. That's all they'd need."

"I won't say anything," Ernesto promised. "I swear."

"Me neither," Abel swore.

53

Paul Morales dropped Ernesto and Abel off at their houses, then drove off. Ernesto wasn't sure what to think. Paul loved Beto and Cruz. He loved them like family. Would Paul's loyalty extend to Cruz even if he *did* rob the thrift store? Ernesto was deeply troubled that a guy was out there who was willing to hold a gun on a clerk. If that guy was Cruz, then the right thing to do would be to alert the police. But Ernesto had promised not to talk about what he saw. And he would keep his promise.

Still, he was deathly afraid that the robber would strike again in a few more days. What if it turned out to be Cruz Lopez behind the gun? What if he fired it and hurt or killed somebody? Ernesto knew he would never forgive himself for as long as he lived. The possibility of that haunted him now. It weighed him down like a stone hung from his neck.

The Vasquezes arrived at eleven thirty on Sunday for dinner at the Sandoval house. Eva Vasquez was a lovely woman, perfectly coiffed and well dressed. Her husband was a pleasant-looking, rumpled man. His demeanor suggested that he generally obeyed his wife.

Maria Sandoval had made a nice dinner. It featured all the foods Eva Vasquez liked and none she did not approve of. The Vasquezes had long since rejected most Mexican favorites like *carne asada*, *quesadillas*, *tacos*, *tamales*, and refried beans. Except for their surname, nobody would have guessed their ancestry. They enjoyed popular and classical music. Latin sounds repelled them. They deliberately joined a church in Los Angeles that had few Hispanics and no mass in Spanish on the schedule. Ernesto wondered whether they even remembered the Spanish language they had spoken as children. Ernesto himself was very proud of being bilingual.

Grandma Eva hugged her daughter, then backed up and looked at her figure. It had changed to accommodate the baby.

"Oh Maria, you look so—" she started to say.

"Pregnant," Ernesto's mother finished the sentence. "Just wait a few more weeks, and then you'll really see big mama."

"Oh dear!" *Abuela* Eva sighed, as if the coming of the new child was a mixed blessing.

"Hello Ernie," Grandma said. "Your mother said you were running for senior class president at your school. That's wonderful. I just know you'll win." She turned to the little girls then, hugging them. Finally she turned to her son-in-law and smiled thinly. She would never quite forgive this man for crushing the dreams she had for her only child.

They dined on shrimp salad with watercress and other leafy green vegetables. A delicious minestrone soup and a lemon cake completed the meal. As the dinner progressed, Grandma Eva inquired, "So Maria, you were writing a new book. It's about piglets, am I right?"

"Not piglets, Mom, pandas," Maria Sandoval corrected her. "You know, those big cute bears from China? The Chinese loan them to zoos in America. When they produce cubs, we're allowed to keep the cubs until they're grown. But then they must return to China. My story is about a panda who goes through this experience. It's sort of a story about change, how animals and people—"

"This is another children's book?" Grandma Eva cut in, a look of disappointment on her face.

"Yes Mom," Mom replied, "I love to write them. We have this awesome artist who—"

"But there is so much more prestige in, for example, books for teenagers," Eva interrupted again. "Even older children like those Harry Potter books . . ."

Juanita was getting bored with the adult conversation and piped up. "Grandma, we have a new hamster in our classroom. His name is Hammurabi."

"Daddy said Hammurabi was a great lawyer like Uncle Arturo," Katalina added. "Daddy knows all that stuff about famous people. Daddy's smart."

"I'm sure he is," Grandma Eva said sourly.

After dinner, they sat in the living room, drinking coffee and hot chocolate. Ernesto realized that his grandfather had not spoken a single sentence since they arrived. Other than "Pass the salt," he was silent. Now, as he sipped his coffee, he spoke. "Just think, by this time next year little Alfredo will be starting to stand up."

"They'll name the child Alfred," Grandma Eva declared. "Not Alfredo. Alfred sounds more American."

"Actually," Mom responded, "we plan to have him christened Alfredo. That's my dad's name."

"Everyone will call him Al or Fred, won't they, dear?" Grandma asked in a testy voice. She looked at her husband and remarked, "Everyone calls you Al."

"Yes," *Abuelo* Alfredo admitted. Then, in a moment of rare courage, he said, "But it would be wonderful if he was christened Alfredo, just as I was. Wonderful."

"Whatever," Grandma conceded. She glared at Ernesto's father, then at her own daughter. "You know," she declared, "I welcome this new baby with as much joy as everyone else. But the fourth child is going to change your life so much, Maria. At this stage of your life, you had a golden opportunity to recover some of your lost dreams." Grandma Eva reached over and grasped her daughter's arm. "To finally get that college education, to blossom as you were meant to do . . ."

"I'm very happy right where I am," Ernesto's mother stated. "I cannot imagine my life being any happier."

Ernesto's father looked over at his wife with deep love and appreciation. Ernesto could always see the affection between his parents. You couldn't miss it. They seemed as much in love now as they must have been years ago when they were very young.

"Darling," Grandma lectured, "I know you think you are happy, and that is wonderful. But sometimes we accept less because we have settled for less. At our church in Los Angeles, we were encouraged to adopt a poor child in El Salvador and to contribute to the child's family. We adopted a little girl who lives in a tin house in squalor. She writes us letters telling us how happy she is with her mother and father and four siblings. They are, of course, grateful for our help. They say they are happy, but of course they're not. How could they be happy without a decent house, a car, nice furnishings? They have nothing. But they think they are happy because they don't know what they're missing. In a similar way—"

This time Maria Sandoval cut into her mother's words. "Mom, if this is not happiness here with Luis, and Ernie, Katalina and Juanita—if this is not happiness, then there is no such thing as happiness in the world."

Ernesto almost stood up and applauded. His mother had told his grandmother how happy she was right here with her family. The rest of the evening was spent with Grandma Eva looking at rough drafts of Mom's new book on pandas.

"The young panda grew up here in the States," Maria Sandoval explained. "Then suddenly she had to part with all her friends. She to be put on a strange airplane and go to a place she had not seen before—China. But after she landed, she made wonderful new friends. It's all about being willing to say good-bye to one life and hello to a new one. It's like our kids leaving LA after ten years and fitting in around here, Mom."

Katalina spoke up. "Yeah Grandma, I liked our house in Los Angeles. I had lots of friends. I was sad to leave everybody and move here. I thought I'd never have as much fun as I had in second grade. But now I'm in third grade, and it's even funner."

Grandma Eva frowned. "'Funner' is not a word," she declared. Eva Vasquez and her husband lived in a lovely gated community in Los Angeles County. She felt bad that her daughter lived in a modest home on Wren Street in the same *barrio* that the Vasquezes had eagerly put behind them.

To Maria, *Abuela* said, "All parents want their children to do a little better than they did, to rise a little higher, Maria. But sometimes it seems you are going backward . . ." She shrugged. "But it's not my place to say so."

"You've already said it," Ernesto thought.

The visit wound down. Ernesto was glad when his grandparents put on their coats and went to their car for the drive up north. Grandma Eva upset him because she made Mom feel bad. And poor Grandpa Alfredo was almost nonexistent, sitting beside his wife like a poodle. Ernesto thought how strange life was. In Naomi's house, Felix Martinez was the boss, and Linda Martinez was the meek, submissive partner. It was the opposite in the Vasquez house. Ernesto liked how things were in his parents' house. Sometimes his parents argued but never in a mean way. And then they came to a compromise. Neither Mom nor Dad was the boss. They were partners. Ernesto wanted it to be that way when he had a family of his own.

CHAPTER FOUR

Ernesto couldn't sleep well that night. He kept thinking of the holdup at the thrift store. He kept thinking about Cruz Lopez. Was he running from the scene of the crime? The robbery wouldn't have bothered Ernesto so much if the thief hadn't used a gun. Why hadn't the robber just rushed in, grabbed some stuff, and beat it out of there? That wouldn't have bothered Ernesto so much.

The use of a gun changed everything. It turned something bad into something horrible. Guys who pointed a gun at another human being were dangerous. Guys who used guns to stick up places didn't do it just once. Even if they didn't fire the gun one time, they might fire it the next time. The poor old lady in the thrift store didn't put up a fight. The clerk in the liquor store might, and he could end up dead.

Ernesto worked for Bashar at the pizzeria. Bashar had often boasted to him that no thief was going to walk off with his hard-earned money. Bashar wouldn't meekly surrender his money. Would an armed robber shoot him for the money?

Ernesto tossed around in bed. He tried to convince himself that he was doing the right thing. He couldn't tell anyone that he'd seen Cruz Lopez running down the street that day. Ernesto had sworn to Paul that he would keep the secret. He couldn't go back on his word.

But Ernesto had to talk to somebody. Abel had heard him tell Paul about seeing Cruz. Ernesto sat up in bed and punched in Abel's cell number.

"Yeah?" Abel answered. He hadn't gone to bed yet. He was in the kitchen trying out a new recipe.

"Abel, I can't sleep," Ernesto told him. "I'm thinking about Cruz Lopez. Do you think he maybe held up the thrift store?"

"I don't know, dude," Abel replied. "It's possible. Paul and me been dropping off groceries at the Lopez house for a while now. Cruz's never there. I know Carmen is scared of him. But she's so much in love with Paul. She just puts up with dudes like Cruz and Beto. If Paul got a pet gorilla, I think she'd put up with it."

"I promised Paul not to tell anybody about seeing Cruz running away that day," Ernesto said. "But Abel, what if Cruz stuck up the store and next time he shoots somebody? How'm I going to feel then?"

"I like Paul," Abel remarked. "He's always been straight with me. My girl, Claudia, she knows Paul a lot better than I do. She worked with him a long time at the donut shop. She said you couldn't have a better friend or a worse enemy than Paul Morales. I wouldn't rat out his friend, Ernie. If you do, and the cops came down on Cruz . . . I wouldn't want to be you, man, not when Paul caught up to you."

"Yeah, I hear you," Ernesto agreed. "I just hope there isn't another robbery. I hope the cops nab the dude who took down the thrift store. And I hope it isn't Cruz."

"Hey Ernie," Abel changed the subject. "That was real cool today. I mean, how you chipped in with Paul and me to help the Lopezes. Paul was blown away by what you did. Your money made a lot of difference."

"I felt good doing it Abel," Ernesto responded. "Did you see inside that fridge in that apartment, man? A carton of milk that was almost empty and a yogurt. The cupboard was even worse. I look at the fridge in our house. There's so much stuff I can't even find what I want. It must be awful to come home, and there's nothing to eat. That's especially bad for kids."

"Yeah," Abel said.

By the time Ernesto hung up, he felt a little better. He was grateful to have Abel to talk with. Abel Ruiz was his first friend at Cesar Chavez High School and his best friend. Abel was willing to trust in Paul's judgment about Cruz. Abel was willing to take a leap of faith. Ernesto figured he had no choice but to do the same.

At school the next day, Carmen Ibarra approached Ernesto.

Ernesto recalled how Carmen and Paul Morales first met. Paul had seen her in the red convertible she received as a seventeenth birthday gift from her parents. He'd yelled to his friends that the car was hot but that the driver was hotter. It was the first time a guy had come on so strong to Carmen. It didn't hurt that Paul was very handsome and had an irresistible bad-boy charm. Paul and Carmen had been together ever since.

"Hey Ernie, me and Paul went out last night," Carmen said. "He told me what you did—kicking in bucks to help that poor family. Paul was really touched by that. You went up in his book, I'm telling you."

"Oh, I didn't do that much," Ernesto objected. "But we did buy a lot of food. You know, the poor families that live on Starling do most of their shopping at the little mini mall markets. Stuff is expensive there. You get a lot more for your money at the supermarket. But they can't go to the supermarket 'cause it's too far away to walk. The Lopez family doesn't even have a car. At the supermarket, we got like three pounds of oranges for the price of one pound at the mini mall. And there were bargains on spaghetti and ground beef."

"I talked to my dad about the Lopez family," Carmen told Ernesto. "He's going to make some phone calls. They should at least be getting food stamps."

"That's good," Ernesto said. "Cruz Lopez has a real good friend in Paul. He couldn't think more of him if they were brothers."

"Yeah," Carmen agreed. Suddenly, she didn't look very happy. "You know, once me and Paul were out driving. We saw the

69

police busting Cruz and Beto. Paul insisted on stopping and demanding to know from the officers what was going on. Cruz and Beto were handcuffed and everything. And there was Paul arguing with the cops. I got so scared. All I saw was me and Paul ending up arrested too. Finally the cops got Paul to move along, but then he came back. Turns out it Cruz forgot to get the new tags put on the license plate. Paul was steamed. He went on and on about his good friends getting hassled for no reason." Carmen shook her head.

"When we dropped the food at the Lopez house," Ernesto told her, "Cruz wasn't there. The Dad said Cruz hadn't been around for days. He sounded worried. Did Paul say anything about that?"

"Yeah," Carmen replied. "Paul said when he gets off work at the computer store, he's going to look for Cruz. He's checked with Beto. But Beto hasn't seen him for a while either. Paul said Cruz is real depressed that he can't help his family more. He's really down on himself. He's like twenty and going nowhere fast."

"They're high school dropouts, right? Cruz and Beto both?" Ernesto asked.

"Yeah sure, well duh!" Carmen groaned. "They've been out of school since tenth grade. Paul hooked up with them when he was a senior at Chavez. They met playing video games at an arcade."

"That's why my dad works so hard to keep kids in school," Ernesto responded. "He walks the *barrio*, trying to get the dropouts back off the street. He risks his own safety trying to talk these kids into saving their own lives. Man, if you haven't even got a high school diploma, you're cooked. But, you know, maybe Cruz and Beto could get into community college for GED prep or tech training. Maybe they could learn a trade or something."

"Paul's been pushing them to get a GED," Carmen said. "But, you know, once you drop out, you start taking lousy jobs. Then it's hard to get back on the bicycle.

71

That's what makes Paul so special, why I respect him so much. He had a rough time growing up, shunted around half a dozen foster homes. His mom died on drugs. His dad ignored him. But he never dropped out. He kept on going to school. Now he's at the community college taking those filmmaking classes. He says the teacher there really likes him. She thinks he has a bright future."

"So," Ernesto asked, "Paul's gonna be hunting for Cruz?"

"Yeah," Carmen confirmed. "He's gonna tell Cruz that my father, the councilman, is onboard now. They're getting help for the family. That might cheer Cruz up and get him home."

Carmen smiled at Ernesto. "Anyway, big guy, I really admire how much you care about people. That's why so many of us here at school love you. You're going to make the best senior class president ever." Ernesto gave Carmen a hug.

By the end of the school day, Ernesto had made up his mind. Tonight, after work, he would talk to his father about Cruz and Beto. Ernesto wouldn't bring up his suspicions about the thrift store robbery. He'd promised Paul he wouldn't do that. But Dad felt strongly about saving kids in the *barrio*. Maybe he could do something for Cruz and Beto. They were too old for high school. But Luis Sandoval knew someone in the admissions department at the community college. Maybe he could make a call.

After work that night, Ernesto and his father took a walk. They often walked together. Their walks were the best time to talk. For some reason, Ernesto found it easier to talk to his father on their walks. They talked a lot about dropouts and gang wannabes. When Mom heard talk like that, she got nervous. She was worried about Dad's venturing into the *barrio* in search of kids to save.

"Dad," Ernesto began, "my friend Paul Morales has sort of lost track of his pal, Cruz Lopez. He dropped out of school a long time ago. The guy's about twenty—

shaved head, tattoos, oversized clothes. His family is in trouble, and he's sort of missing."

"Lopez . . . Lopez . . ." Luis Sandoval repeated the name. "Oh yeah. That's the family Emilio is trying to help. Emilio and my brother, your Uncle Arturo, they're trying to help. They are trying to get the government's wheels turning for these people. They've sort of fallen through the cracks. That's Cruz's family?"

"Yeah, Dad," Ernesto responded. "Cruz has this crummy job cleaning up at a construction site. He's feeling like he's letting his family down. So he's hiding out."

"Well," Dad said, "I was planning to play some basketball over at Chavez. I've got a couple guys thinking about coming back to school. One of the guys is real savvy about the underbelly of the *barrio*. I'll ask him about Cruz. Maybe he knows where the kid is holed up."

"Okay if I tag along, Dad?" Ernesto asked.

"Sure, that's fine," Dad answered with a grin. "I don't think you ever met Sal Lupo. He's quite a character. Only fifteen years old, but street smart in a scary way. Has the old street cred. I think it would be best if we told your mom we just took a longer walk. She doesn't like it when I spend too much time at basketball. I don't think she likes the dudes I play with."

They stopped back at the house. Luis told Maria Sandoval that their walk would be longer tonight and pulled on a sweater. "Me and Ernie enjoy the good night air. Helps clear our minds. Nothing like a good long talk between a father and son when the stars are shining," Dad remarked.

"Yeah," Mom responded, seeing right through the ploy. "Then maybe shoot a few baskets with the gang wannabes."

"Well, we might do a couple of hoops," Dad admitted.

"Just be careful, Luis," Mom advised. "I really am proud of you for what you're doing. But I'm scared too. You're such a good person. Sometimes I don't think you realize the kind of people who're out there."

They walked over to the basketball hoops at Cesar Chavez High School. About half a dozen kids were already there. "There's Sal," Dad said. He pointed out a chunky boy. The kid was amazingly accurate in the free throws, even though he was pretty short. Most of the boys were lean and tall.

"Hey Sal, way to go!" Luis Sandoval shouted.

The boy turned and walked over to Ernesto and his father. When Sal Lupo was close enough, Ernesto saw the ugly white scar on his dark left cheek. The scar disfigured the side of his face. It was a zigzag burn scar. It didn't look that bad. But it was the first thing you noticed about Sal Lupo, even more than the extra weight he carried.

"This is my son, Ernie," Luis Sandoval said. "Ernie, this is my buddy, Sal. He's coming back to Chavez High any day now."

"In your dreams, man," Sal sneered.

"Sal's a computer genius," Dad went on, ignoring the boy's negative remark. "All he needs is a good education, and he'll take off like a rocket. He'll go right to the top. Get to be king of the geeks."

"I don't want no good education," Sal objected. "I'm learnin' all I need to know right here on the streets." Sal looked at Ernesto and said, "Your father's a good man, Ernie. But right now he don't know what he's talking about. School's a trap, and this mouse ain't takin' the bait."

"What's wrong with school, Sal?" Ernesto asked. "You get bored or something? Lotta real smart guys get bored in school. But we got a young science and math teacher at Chavez now, a fabulous dude. José Cabral. You'd like him. He'd be happy to have you."

"They always had names for me," Sal Lupo responded. "Like lard butt. That was one of the nicer ones. Then I had the accident. I got a new name. Scarface—*cara cortada*."

"Not everybody calls you names, Sal," Luis Sandoval told him. "Only the creeps. You can't let the creeps ruin your life, Sal. That's giving them way too much power."

"Yeah, you can't let them win," Ernesto chimed in. "Ignore them. Laugh in their faces. Then when you're hauling in big bucks, you'll have the last laugh. You know what they say, Sal. A good life is the best revenge on all those people who try to sink your boat."

"You got yourself a Mini-Me here, Mr. Sandoval," Sal remarked, smiling a little. "He's just like you, but that ain't bad . . ."

"Sal," Dad said, changing the subject, "we're looking for a kid with problems."

"Tell 'im to join the club," Sal quipped. "We all got problems."

"This kid," Ernesto continued, "his name is Cruz Lopez. His family is really in trouble. He got bummed out because he couldn't help them. So he left home. He's dropped out of sight, and his friends are worried about him. He's got a shaved head and tattoos. We want to get hold of him. He needs to know a lot of people are helping his family now. He needs to come home."

"I know who you're talking about," Sal Lupo responded. "He's *seriously* bummed out."

"Know where he's at?" Ernesto asked.

"Sure," Sal affirmed. "The far east end of the ravine. Not down in the ravine where the old guys hang out. The kids go to the rough, brushy part. It's called Turkey Neck 'cause the path down is all twisty and narrow. You can't see the camp from the street. That's one of the things about it."

"How do we find the place?" Ernesto asked. His dad glanced at Ernesto when he "we." But he said nothing.

"The path runs off Washington, where it hooks up with Starling," Sal said. "You keep goin'. Pretty soon you get to this bunch of plastic bags and blankets." Sal looked at Mr. Sandoval and then his son. "It's kinda rough down there. Some of the dudes got knives. You can smell the weed right away."

"Thanks, Sal," Dad said warmly. "And I'm not giving up on you. You're going to be in the sophomore class in a few more weeks. You'll be taking math and science with José Cabral. You're gonna wonder why you didn't go back sooner."

"Dream on!" Sal responded.

"No dreams, Sal." Mr. Sandoval wagged a finger at the boy. "I'm gonna get you. I'm gonna bring you to Cesar Chavez High School. There's no doubt about it. You can run, Sal, but you can't hide. Not from me," Dad snickered.

Sal Lupo looked at Ernesto. "He always like this?" he asked.

"Yeah," Ernesto replied. "And he's always right too."

CHAPTER FIVE

Ernesto and his father walked away from the basketball court. Ernesto pulled out his cell phone and called Paul Morales. "Hey Paul," he said, "Dad and I are walking home from the basketball court. I think we know where Cruz is. Dad has a friend who knows the *barrio* pretty well. He's seen Cruz at a camp in the ravine."

"Good deal!" Paul exclaimed. "Give it to me."

"It's the east end of the ravine, the brushy part," Ernesto replied. "The trail down leads from the intersection of Washington and Starling."

"Turkey Neck," Paul responded. "You mean he's hanging with that crowd? That's not so cool."

"This dude my father knows says he's seriously bummed out," Ernesto explained.

"Thanks Ernie," Paul said. "I'll get over there right away."

"Let me have the phone," Dad requested. Ernesto handed it to his father. Luis Sandoval said, "We're almost home, Paul. We're getting the Volvo and driving over there now too. We'll meet you there."

"Hey man," Paul objected. "I don't want you guys getting mixed up in this. Sometimes there's ugly stuff down there."

"It's okay, Paul," Luis Sandoval replied. "I've been to worse places than Turkey Neck. I've been to places so nasty that guys were trying to blow your head off on every street corner."

They got back to Wren Street within minutes. In the driveway, Ernesto asked, "You sure you want to do this, Dad?"

"Yeah," Dad asserted. "Paul might need some backup. Who knows what condition this Cruz's in. He might not come willingly, you know?"

About two minutes after Ernesto and his father arrived at the trailhead on Washington, Paul drove up in his pickup. Ernesto and his father got out of the Volvo. "Paul, this is my dad. I don't think you ever met him," Ernesto said.

Paul held out his hand. "Nice to meet Ernie's pop," he responded. He noticed the scar on the man's face. "War souvenir?" he asked.

"Yep," Dad said. "IED."

"Iraq or Afghanistan?" Paul asked.

"Iraq. I was part of the surge," Luis Sandoval explained.

"Glad you got back okay, man," Paul told him.

"You and me both," Ernesto's father affirmed wryly.

The trio started down Turkey Neck. It was a narrow, overgrown trail leading to the camp. Runaway kids hung out here. Some stayed for just a night or a few days. Some stayed forever. A seventeen-year-old had overdosed down here last year. After they took the body away, the city had the camp torn up and cleaned out. But a few weeks later, everyone and everything came back.

"What do you guys want?" A harsh voice barked from the darkness. "You cops?"

"No man, chill." Paul spoke in a calm, friendly voice. "We're friends of Cruz Lopez. His old man is hurtin' bad 'bout his boy being gone. The family's in a world of hurt anyway without this. His mom's sick, maybe dying. Cruz needs to come home."

A face emerged from the darkness. It was young face that looked very old. Paul went on. "Cruz, he's my bro. He's as close as blood to me. I want to get the dude home. I got no problems with anybody else down here. I'm just a child of God doing the best he can, *amigo*."

The boy in the darkness swept the beam of a flashlight across Paul Morales's face. He seemed to recognize Paul. He swept Paul's hand with the flashlight beam. Then he turned to speak to others behind him in the darkness. "It's okay. It's the Snake." The kid seemed to relax.

Ernesto had never heard Paul Morales described as "the Snake." Apparently, he was better known down here than Ernesto knew. Ernesto thought about Carmen and her father, Emilio Zapata Ibarra. Mr. Ibarra wasn't crazy about his daughter dating Paul Morales in the first place. What if the councilman were down here now in the murky ravine? What if he were to sniff the smell of grass hanging in the air like fog? He would go ballistic to see how comfortable Paul was in such a place.

The kid with the flashlight led Paul to a shaved head in a sleeping bag. Paul recognized the tattoo. "Hey Cruz! Time to go home, dude," Paul said softly.

Cruz Lopez rose slowly from the bag. Then he saw Ernesto and his father. "Who're *they*?" he asked in a guarded voice.

"*Mis compadres, amigo*," Paul answered. "Come on, man. You need to go home."

Cruz slowly got to his feet. "They don' need me there," he whined. "I can't do nothin' for 'em. They're eatin' dry corn flakes three times a day. I'm supposed to be a man, and I can't do squat for 'em."

"No," Ernesto spoke up. "Paul and Abel and I brought a lot of groceries over there. They're okay now. The biggest problem they got is missing you. We got some friends—a councilman and a lawyer—working to get you guys some real help. You'll all be okay until your dad is called back to work. Things are looking up."

Cruz Lopez looked at Paul. Cruz didn't trust many people in the world, but he trusted Paul. He surely did not trust the well dressed teenager and the older guy he was with. "Paul," Cruz asked, "is the stuff this dude is saying true? Or is it all BS?"

"It's the truth, *amigo*," Paul assured him. "These are my homies man. Your family's gonna be all right. You just need to be home with them."

"I can't go home like this," Cruz objected. "I'm filthy!"

"Yeah, you don't smell so good, dude," Paul sniffed, laughing. "But you can come home with me. You know, my palatial apartment! You can shower. I'll give you some clean clothes. Come on, man. Time to go."

Cruz gathered up his sleeping bag and walked toward his buddy. Paul turned to Ernesto and his father. "Thanks Ernie. Mr. Sandoval. Thanks for giving me the heads-up on this. I never thought Cruz was down so bad that he'd come here. I can't tell you how much your help meant to me."

Paul looked intently at Mr. Sandoval and spoke. "I don't know if Ernie told you. Me and Beto and Cruz were hiking in the Anza-Borrego last year. I got bitten by a rattler. Cruz carried me to meet the paramedics. If he didn't do that, I'd proba-bly have died out there." Paul put his hand on Cruz's shoulder. "This kid saved my life, him and Beto. They aren't just friends.

They're *mis hermanos*. And you know what else, Ernie? You and your dad—you're *mis hermanos* too."

Back at the head of the trail, Ernesto and his father left in the Volvo. The pickup disappeared down the dark street.

"Well, we did a good night's work," Luis Sandoval declared. "That family will be glad to see their boy. I know that Felix Martinez is a different person. He just needed to be reconciled with his two sons. I ran into him the other day while he was walking Brutus. He was actually cordial!" Dad chuckled.

"Yeah," Ernesto agreed. "He even compliments his wife now on her cooking. He used to call everything she made 'slop.' " Ernesto usually talked over his problems with his father. But he couldn't share his misgivings about Cruz. That would be breaking faith with Paul.

At Cesar Chavez High School the next day, Ernesto picked up a copy of the school newspaper, *Adelante*. It had nice photos of the students running for senior class offices.

"Look at that handsome dude there in the middle," Naomi pointed, surprising Ernesto. He didn't even know she had come up behind him. "Is that a babe, or what?"

Ernesto turned and smiled at Naomi. "It's a pretty good picture," Ernesto granted. "I should have gotten a haircut before it was taken. I look like I have a raccoon sitting on my head."

"Oh Ernie," Naomi laughed. "I love your nice mop."

"Good picture of Mira Nuñez too," Ernesto noted.

"Yeah," Naomi agreed. "She's pretty all right. But she has one major drawback. I don't think she can overcome it."

"What's that?" Ernesto asked. Mira was smart, pretty, and friendly. That was a pretty good combination. Everybody seemed to think she'd done a good job as junior class vice president too.

"Clay Aguirre," Naomi stated. "Being connected to him is a major problem. The campaign isn't supposed to start for two weeks. Then we're only supposed to campaign for one week. But Clay is already going around promoting Mira and running you down. He just makes me sick. The only upside is that he makes a lot of other kids sick too. Clay is so obnoxious that he's doing Mira more harm than good."

Ernesto was prepared for lunchtime today. Mom had packed some really delicious *chorizo* sandwiches. She'd even included a nice fresh peach and a little container of homemade chocolate pudding. Ernesto opened his lunch bag with anticipation. He felt as though he was eating like a king. Even Abel and Julio cast envious eyes on Ernesto's lunch.

The boys started talking about which teams would be playing in the Super Bowl this year. Then other voices floated down from the campus. Clay Aguirre was accosting students as they came by. Mira Nuñez was with him. She didn't seem too happy with the strategy. But apparently Clay had talked her into it. She was also saying a few words about her candidacy. Neither Clay nor Mira saw the five boys eating lunch behind the eucalyptus trees.

"Hey there," Clay called. "You're a junior, right?" The boys eating lunch couldn't see whom Clay was talking to, but they heard the voices.

"Yeah," a girl's voice replied.

"You got any idea who you'll be voting for as senior class president?" Clay asked. "This is gonna be an important year for us. We want somebody good. You know Mira here, right? She's junior vice president now, and she's been doing an awesome job. You ready to do the same as senior class president, right, Mira?"

"Uh huh," Mira replied. She sounded embarrassed.

"It says in the *Adelante* that you're not supposed to be campaigning yet," the girl said. "How come you guys are out here?"

"We're not campaigning," Clay protested. "We're just sort of introducing the students to Mira here. Once you get to know Mira, you won't want anybody else. Anyway, the two guys running for senior class president are big losers. This dude Garcia is an egghead. He doesn't care about anything but saving bottles for recycling and stuff. The other one, this Ernesto Sandoval, is even worse. He just blew in here in his junior year. Nobody knows him. He's a real creep, not very friendly, and real arrogant."

Julio Avila started laughing, and Dom and Carlos were shaking their heads. Abel was laughing too. Ernesto was just enjoying his sandwich.

"I got a friend—Yvette Ozono," the girl stated. "She told me Ernesto Sandoval and his father just about saved her life. She said she'd dropped out of school and stuff. And her boyfriend had just been killed. She'd given up on life. She didn't even want to wake up anymore."

The boys heard Clay start to interrupt with, "Yeah, but . . ."

The girl ignored him and kept on talking. "Then Mr. Sandoval and his son helped her get back in school. They turned her whole life around. Yvette said she'd never met a kid who cared more about people than Ernesto. So I don't know what you're talking about."

"Come on, Clay, let's go eat lunch," Mira suggested. "Let's just *go*."

"You guys," the girl continued, "it really stinks what you're doing. This is unfair and dirty campaigning. The adults smear people in the big political campaigns for president and stuff. But we're supposed to be better than that. Now you're making our little school election dirty like the national campaigns."

"I didn't know Clay was going to say all that," Mira explained in a worried voice. "Clay, come on! Let's go!"

But Clay was not finished. "That girl, Yvette Ozono," he declared. "You don't want to believe anything she says. She's a dirty gangbanger girl. She hung out with a murderer named Coyote. The Sandovals weren't doing us any favors bringing trash like her back to school."

"Yvette Ozono is the best math student in Mr. Cabral's class," the girl snapped. "She was on the Chavez math team that went north and won the regional trophy. You're full of it, dude. I don't know you, Mira Nuñez. But you can't have much sense hanging with a jerk like this guy. You're sure not who I want for senior class president."

"You got a big mouth, girl, and you're a dog too," Clay snarled.

"Clay!" Mira almost screamed.

"Shut up, dummy!" Clay snapped at her. "If you were any good at promoting yourself, I wouldn't have to do this. But you're like a zombie. You're gonna lose the election to that creep Sandoval! And it's gonna be your fault."

Ernesto had finished his sandwich. He got up and stepped out from behind the eucalyptus trees. He had recognized the voice of the girl who put Clay in his place. She was in Ms. Hunt's class. "Hey Rosa," he said. "Want half my peach?"

Rosa grinned. "Wow, that's a beautiful peach."

"Yeah, it's big enough for two," Ernesto suggested.

"This isn't a campaign bribe, is it, Ernie?" Rosa asked.

"Yep!" Ernesto replied, cutting the peach in two and handing a half to Rosa.

Mira Nuñez was dragging Clay Aguirre away. Neither of them was looking back.

After school, Ernesto jogged over to Carmen Ibarra's house. She was working on his campaign slogans. Candidates were allowed to plaster the campus with their posters, but only during campaign week. The messages were supposed to be brief and positive.

Carmen had a stack of posters edged in red, white, and blue. She put them on the dining room table. Ernesto flipped through them. "Soar with Sandoval" . . . "For Senior Spirit, It's Sandoval" . . . "Sandoval stands tall. He'll work with one and all." The rest of the slogans were as good or better.

"Wow!" Ernesto exclaimed. "They're so good! I'm humbled. You're so nice to be doing this."

"Dom and Carlos are painting a big poster for the spot in the library. Ernie, I've seen it, and it's beautiful!" Carmen told him.

Emilio Zapata Ibarra came into the room. He was working hard in his new role as councilman. "Hey Ernie," he greeted him. "We're making good progress helping the Lopez family. They're gonna get food stamps for one thing. But the really good news is about his health insurance."

Mr. Ibarra's eyes twinkled. "One of my staff guys went to the construction company where Mr. Lopez worked. You know they told him when he was laid off that his health insurance stopped. That was a lie. It's right in their contract. The coverage continues for the employee and the family for six months after a layoff. So the Lopezes have health insurance. What's more, we might get it extended by threatening to press charges. The construction company broke the law."

The councilman grew serious. "I didn't realize how sick Mrs. Lopez is. She really needs to go see a doctor. They were gonna do an MRI. But she cancelled 'cause she thought there was no health insurance. Now she can go in right away and get herself taken care of."

"That's great, Mr. Ibarra," Ernesto said. "My dad and I and Paul found Cruz last night. He was real depressed that he couldn't help his family. He was hanging out at that camp in the ravine. Paul got him home. The family's dealing with enough stress without their son being missing."

A troubled look came to Mr. Ibarra's face. Ernesto thought he saw a tiny twitch of his mustache. "I know," the father said, "that my beloved *hija* here is in love with

97

Paul Morales. And I know the young man has many good qualities. Apparently, he has a generous heart, which I value very much. But . . ."

"Daddy," Carmen interrupted, wanting to change the subject. "Look at this new poster I just made. 'Seniors: Answer the call for Sandoval!' "

"Yes, very nice, very nice," Mr. Ibarra commented, turning for a second toward his daughter. "Ernie is a fine young man. It would be wonderful for the school if he became senior class president."

Mr. Ibarra turned his attention again to Ernesto. "But on the subject of Paul, he seems to have some very strange friends. I have nothing but sympathy for the poor Lopez family. And we're all working to help them. But this Cruz is a tough character. His friend, Beto Ortiz, is the same. They have shaved heads and tattoos. Paul himself has that snake tattooed on his hand. I mean—what is that? How is this young man going to get a good job when he goes in for an interview? The personnel fellow cannot miss a snake on the young man's hand."

"Paul is doing great in his community college classes, Daddy," Carmen explained. "He's already won a five hundred dollar prize for the short film he wrote and directed. There are thirty students in the filmmaking class. And the teacher is this very wonderful lady—Anisa Lee. Well, she chose just four students to take to the Sundance Film Festival in Park City, Utah. Paul was one of them."

Carmen waited for a reaction from her father, but it didn't come. She went on. "He was so thrilled and excited. It was a real honor for him. Paul is headed for a wonderful career in making films. He wants to be an independent filmmaker, and that field is just exploding now. In that business, it doesn't matter if you have tattoos and stuff."

Ernesto wanted to help Carmen, especially since she was making all his campaign posters. "In fact," he chimed in, "being a little unusual, like, you know, having a snake tattoo. Well, that's sort of a plus in that business. Those movie people like the bizarre . . ."

"Ernesto," Mr. Ibarra said patiently, "you are a splendid young man. But you are not helping here. I am a concerned father. You are not helping me. I am trying to convince my daughter to take a more realistic view of her . . . friend."

"He's helping *me*, Daddy," Carmen said, giggling.

Mr. Ibarra continued to look troubled. He was never happy about his daughter dating Paul Morales. His elder daughter, Lourdes, did not add to his confidence. She told her father that Paul "creeped her out." He certainly didn't seem like the kind of a young man who would fit into the Ibarra family.

Emilio Ibarra had dreamed of his lovely, smart, and vivacious daughter finding a nice, solid young man. He pictured someone like Ernesto Sandoval or even Abel Ruiz. It was not a father's fondest wish that his daughter date such a man. Paul came from a severely dysfunctional family. As a boy, he was shuffled through a series of bad foster homes. His mother died of a drug overdose. His father was absent entirely. Perhaps the worst part had to do with Paul's brother, David. He was now an inmate at the nearby prison, serving time for burglary.

Cruz Lopez and Beto Ortiz only compounded the problem. Accepting Paul Morales himself was bad enough. His manner was brash and aggressive. He spoke in street slang. A snake was tattooed on the back of his hand. It was a big leap of faith for Emilio Ibarra to accept Paul as his daughter's loved one.

But Paul called Cruz and Beto his "homies." They only made matters worse. They frightened Mr. Ibarra to the core of his being. Ernesto Sandoval was not unsympathetic. He understood how the father felt.

CHAPTER SIX

The next day at school, Ernesto noticed something. Clay Aguirre was not shepherding Mira Nuñez around the campus. The couple wasn't campaigning. Ernesto guessed that Mira's confrontation with Rosa, Yvette Ozono's friend, was just too unpleasant. Mira had always caved in to most of Clay's ideas. But yesterday was probably too much. Maybe Mira did something she never had done. She refused to obey Clay. She stuck to her guns.

Ernesto was at the vending machine. He was trying to decide what he wanted. A vegetable juice had a combination of juice: celery, beets, parsley, lettuce, watercress, and spinach. Ernesto knew this was the healthy choice. But he loved another drink. It was a very sweet carbonated fake orange juice. His brain told him to go for the vegetable juice. But his taste buds screamed for the sticky sweet orange drink. It would be just right for washing down his barbecued beef sandwich.

"I always drink the vegetable juice," said a girl who'd come up beside him. Ernesto didn't immediately recognize Mira Nuñez's voice. "It's really good for you. It has two servings of the vegetables we need every day."

"Yeah," Ernesto admitted. "That's what they say. But I love that orange drink. I've had it before. I tend to like stuff that isn't good for me."

"You sure seem healthy," Mira commented. "You must be doing something right."

"Thanks," Ernesto said. "But I guess bad food habits catch up to you when you get older. I guess the body is more forgiving at our age."

"Ernie," Mira Nuñez remarked, "I can't get over you."

Ernesto looked at the beautiful girl. "*What?*"

"The other day when you and your friends were eating," Mira explained. "You'd heard what Clay was saying about you. He was going on and on. And I was just standing there like I agreed with him. You must have been furious. Yet here you are, nice and polite, as if nothing happened. I don't get it, Ernie."

Ernesto shrugged. "Oh, I'm used to Clay doing stuff like that. Actually, I sort of hate him, to be honest. I've felt that way for a long time. I know you're not supposed to hate anybody. I tell myself I really don't hate him. But then 'myself' tells me I'm a liar."

Ernesto fed his coins into the machine and picked the orange drink. It clunked down to the tray, where Ernesto retrieved it. "Anyway," he went on, "I know what Clay is. I know what he does, and I don't expect any different. But I didn't blame you for what was going on. I'm with Naomi Martinez, you know. She's the best thing that ever happened to me. I love her with all my heart. But she used to date Clay Aguirre. She dated him for a long time. I guess she must have seen something good in him. I guess maybe you do too. So I'm not judging. But what you see in him sure beats me."

"I know when Clay first started dating me," Mira admitted, "he did it just to make Naomi jealous. I knew that, but still I was so thrilled. I watch him playing football. I watch him taking on tacklers, hitting hard. It just sends chills up my spine. He almost seems like a mythical creature, the way he can zigzag and get the ball into the end zone. He's the best football player with the Cougars. He makes plays that no one else can."

"Well, he is good at the game," Ernesto admitted.

"It's not just that," Mira went on, smiling. "I know that Clay cares about me now.

He really does. He'll surprise me with a single rose. He seems to care for me more each day. It makes me so happy when he's in a good mood. We like to go to a scary movie and we snuggle . . ."

To himself, Ernesto commented, "Yeah, he calls you 'stupid' and 'dummy' when he's in a bad mood. That sure is proof that he cares about you." But to Mira, Ernesto said, "If he makes you happy, Mira, well, that's your call. I wish you the best."

Mira smiled again. "You're a great guy, Ernie. Naomi is a lucky girl. I just want you to know that if you become senior class president, I won't be mad at you. You're sort of charismatic. I know a lot of kids who look up to you. Clay said nobody likes you, but that's not true. A lot of kids do."

"Thanks, Mira," Ernesto responded. "And if you win, I won't be mad either. We'll make a deal. Whoever wins, the loser will be okay with it."

"Cool," Mira said. Then she looked hesitant. "Ernie, I know you don't talk to

Clay much anymore. But if you do, I'd appreciate it if he never knew we had this conversation."

"Of course," Ernesto agreed. He watched the girl walk away. He felt sorry for her. She was afraid of Clay. She loved him, but she was afraid of him. If Clay found out she had had a cordial conversation with Ernesto, he'd be angry. He'd freeze her out, call her nasty names. Or do worse.

At the end of school that day, Ernesto and Naomi saw Dom Reynosa and Carlos Negrete. The boys were painting a big poster for the library promoting Ernesto as senior class president. Each of the candidates was allowed a poster no larger than four feet square. It would be in the library during campaign week. At the top of the poster, in red, white, and blue colors, was the name "Ernie." Below it was a likeness of Ernesto Sandoval that he considered incredibly flattering.

"I don't really look like that," Ernesto remarked. The guy on the poster was dashing, like a superhero. He was looking out over the campus of Cesar Chavez High School with outstretched arms. Behind him was the beautiful mural of Cesar Chavez that the boys had painted on the science building. At the bottom of the poster was the slogan "*¡Sí, se puede!*" It meant, "Yes, it's possible!" It was the slogan of Cesar Chavez. But Ernesto planned to use it in his campaign speech.

"Oh wow!" Naomi Martinez said. "Who is that guy? Is that really *my* boyfriend? Don't tell me that handsome dude is really mine!"

"Totally," Ernesto responded, laughing. "And I'm saving that poster for when I run for the presidency of the United States."

Ernesto drove Naomi home that day. On the way, he told her about his encounter with Mira Nuñez. "It was really sort of sad," he said when he finished telling Naomi about it.

"It's a wonder such a nice, pretty girl puts up with him," Naomi declared.

Ernesto felt like saying, "You did, babe." But he wouldn't dream of saying anything to hurt Naomi's feelings.

But Naomi said what was on his mind. "I bet you wonder if her dad is like mine. Does she put up with him because her mom puts up with that stuff too? But it's not like that for Mira. Mira lives with her mother. Her parents split up years ago, when Mira was about eight. She told me she adored her father. She was just grief stricken when he left."

Naomi thought for a moment. "The dad found somebody else and just split. He said he wasn't happy where he was. I guess maybe one of those know-it-all psychologists could explain Mira's behavior. He'd maybe say that Mira never understood why her dad abandoned her mom and her. Maybe she feels vulnerable with a boyfriend. She's always afraid of doing the wrong thing and losing him, like she and her mom lost her dad. Mira doesn't seem to trust love . . ."

"Who can say for sure?" Ernesto remarked. They were quiet for a while.

"Well, we made a deal, Mira and I," Ernesto announced. "We won't be mad no matter who wins. She's a nice girl. I wished her luck."

"That's good, Ernie. That's how it should be," Naomi affirmed. "But, of course, I'm sure you'll win."

"Hey Naomi," Ernesto asked abruptly, "how are things going at Chill Out?"

Naomi loved her job at the frozen yogurt shop—Chill Out. Everything had been perfect until Elia Ancho, the father of the manager, lost his mind. He had recently married a young woman, and she fell overboard on a honeymoon cruise. She drowned and was never seen again. In the man's unhinged mind, Naomi was his lost bride. One night, he tried to kidnap her, and only Ernesto's brave act saved her.

"Mr. Ancho is permanently at a hospital in Mexico, the poor man," Naomi reported. "If and when he recovers, he'll be staying in Mexico with his daughters. So I don't have to worry about him anymore. Things are good, Ernie. Jimmy Ancho is a great boss. I love working with Sherry. The customers couldn't be nicer, and I'm making great money. I've got enough money saved, in fact, that I'm looking for a good used car this weekend."

"This is not good news, Naomi," Ernesto complained. "That means you won't be riding with me as much."

"Sure I will," Naomi assured him, "and sometimes you'll be riding with me."

"You're going to get some hot car, aren't you, Naomi?" Ernesto asked. "Something to make my poor Volvo feel bad, to say nothing of how *I'll* feel."

Naomi laughed. "I love your Volvo, Ernie. It's like you. Dependable, faithful, good to the core. I love everything about you, Ernie. I love your crazy hair. And I love your cute dark sweaters with the button at the top always missing. I love your jeans and your oversized sneakers.

I love the way you stand at the vending machine trying to convince yourself to buy the healthy vegetable juice. Then you just end up with that carbonated junk."

"Man, you got my number," Ernesto conceded. "I didn't even think you noticed some of that. Listen, though. Is it okay if I come with you when you buy the car? I'm not an expert on cars, but I could maybe offer a little advice. The main thing is that it's a safe car. It will be carrying the most precious cargo on the planet—you."

"That's sweet, Ernie," Naomi responded. "Of course, you can come along. I'm going to look on Saturday afternoon. You could pick me up around ten. Maybe I'll be riding home in my new wheels."

"You could always get a Volvo too," Ernesto suggested. "I've had such good luck with mine. It would be kinda cute if we both had Volvos." Ernesto glanced over at Naomi. "No deal, huh?"

"No deal," Naomi said.

On Saturday morning, Ernesto and Naomi drove to a used car lot on Washington Street. Naomi was talking excitedly. "I searched the Internet. This place seemed to have the best deals. The new car dealers usually have really expensive newer used cars. You have to go to a place like this to get a car eight or nine years old. Dad was on my case all last night, asking me why I can't just inherit the family Toyota. But I want *my* car."

"Looking for something in particular, Naomi?" Ernesto asked.

"Yeah, sort of, but it's probably gone," Naomi answered. "They got some fairly new cars, but I don't like them. There was this one car that just caught my eye. The blurb said it was 'gorgeous.' It was only eighteen hundred dollars. I can handle that. But it's probably gone."

They pulled into the used car lot and got out of the Volvo. A young man approached them. He smiled broadly and greeted them. "Hello there. Beautiful cars here today.

Cheap. Run good." He looked at Ernesto, ignoring Naomi. "What you got in mind, sir?"

"I'm the one looking for a car," Naomi corrected him. "I'm almost seventeen, and I want my own car."

"How much money you want to spend?" the young man asked.

"Less than two thousand," Naomi replied. She looked around. She saw a lot of Hondas and Toyotas. She saw a few pickups. But she didn't see the car she was looking for. It was described as gold in color. Suddenly Naomi let out a little gasp. "There it is, Ernie! There's my car!" A big smile broke on her face.

"You like that classic Chevy?" the dealer asked. "Yeah, that's a gem. Beautiful car. Very cheap. Runs like a charm. Just eighteen hundred dollars."

Naomi rushed over to the car and walked around it. She sat in it. Then she asked, "May I take it around the block?"

"Yeah, sure," the dealer agreed. "Let me get the keys."

Naomi got behind the wheel of the car, and Ernesto sat beside her. The salesman took a seat in the back. He felt strange being in a car with Naomi and not to be the one driving.

"Oh Ernie," Naomi said, driving slowly down the street. "I love it. It's so smooth. It's got CD, stereo. And it's a four door. I love four doors. If you're taking friends, they don't have to crawl in the back. Oh, I love this car!"

"You going to have a mechanic look it over, Naomi?" Ernesto asked. He spoke loudly enough that he was sure the salesman heard what he said.

Naomi turned the car around and drove back to the used car lot. When they were all out of the car, she asked the dealer whether she could have a mechanic check the car before she bought it.

"Tell you what," the dealer proposed. "We got a three-day return policy, no questions asked. Bring the car back in three days, and you get your money back. During that time, you can have your mechanic check it out."

"Is that in writing?" Ernesto asked, sternly.

"Yeah, come on," the dealer said, leading the way into a small portable office. He put the sales papers out on the desk, and Ernesto read them carefully. "Yeah, Naomi," he affirmed, "it says so here clearly. You can bring the car back within three days and get a full refund."

"If your mechanic finds a problem, you just bring it back," the dealer assured her. "But it's a good car. No problems. She's a sweetheart of a car."

Forty-five minutes later, Naomi was driving the classic Chevy home to Bluebird Street with Ernesto following in his Volvo. Naomi's car was beautiful all right. Ernesto liked it a lot better than his Volvo. But he wasn't going for a different car himself anytime soon. He was saving money for college. As long as the Volvo ran well, he wasn't going to turn the old friend out to pasture.

"Hey," Felix Martinez exclaimed when Naomi drove in. "Look at that!" He turned and yelled, "Linda, come see what the kid bought. She got herself a gold classic Chevy. Hey, that's a beautiful car, little girl. I hope she runs as good as she looks."

Naomi's mother came hurrying out. "Oh Naomi, I just love it!" she cried.

"Dad, I just need for a mechanic to look the car over," Naomi said. "Do you think you could take it somewhere? If something's wrong I can take the car back in three days and get a full refund. Do you know someone who'd look it over, Dad?"

"Hey, sure baby," her father responded. "I'll take it over to Rodrigo right now. When he sees me coming, he clears the decks. He'll get right at it. He'll check the car out and give you an honest report."

Naomi reluctantly yielded the keys to her father. "Thanks, Dad!"

He took the keys and got into the car. As he started it up, he promised, "I'll call ya soon as I get the verdict!"

Then she climbed into Ernesto's Volvo. "Let's go somewhere and celebrate," Naomi suggested. "How about Hortencia's for some *tamales*?"

"Sounds good," Ernesto agreed.

"Oh Ernie," Naomi enthused, "I love that car so much. I hope it's okay. It's just the kind of a car I've dreamed of. I was so afraid it wouldn't be on the lot anymore. I think now that I was meant to have it."

Naomi and Ernesto waited at Hortencia's for the phone call from Naomi's father. In the meantime, they ate *tamales* and drank chocolate shakes.

As time went by, Naomi began to fret. "Oh, I hope everything's okay. It would just break my heart if something was wrong and I had to take the car back."

"That's the nice thing about my Volvo," Ernesto said. "As ugly as it is, everything always works okay."

Hortencia came over to talk to them. "Oscar Perez and his band're coming down next weekend, you guys. Naomi, your brother will be here too. We'll have a Friday night party. You know what Oscar told me, girl? He heard you singing at that school celebration, and he said you got a great voice. Plus you're so pretty. He said if you want to join the band for a few gigs this summer, you're welcome. You won't be busy with school, and you'd make some money. Plus it'd be fun."

"Oh, I'm not a professional. I'd be scared to death," Naomi protested.

"Girl, don't sell yourself short," Hortencia told her. "You've got a really nice voice. You got a lot of range. Listen to some of these singers today on those talent programs. They got these weak little voices. Oscar was really impressed. You think about it, Naomi."

Just then, Naomi's cell phone rang. Naomi's eyes widened, and she stared at Ernesto. "Ohhh! I hope it's good, I hope it's good."

"Hey baby," Felix Martinez said at the other end of the line. "You got a winner here. Rodrigo said it's good to go for at least fifty thousand miles. Everything's ticking just right."

"Thanks Dad!" Naomi cried. "I'll be right home." She turned to Ernesto. "The car is good, Ernie. There's nothing wrong with it. Oh Ernie, I got my car! I got the car of my dreams!"

They got up from the booth, and Ernesto gave Naomi a hug. They said good-bye to Hortencia and walked out to the Volvo for the short ride home.

"We have the old Toyota and Dad's pickup in the garage, Ernie. It's a two-car garage. So I guess I'll have to park my car in the driveway or out on the street. But I hate to do that."

"Maybe you can get one of those car covers for it," Ernesto suggested.

They turned onto Bluebird Street, and Naomi screamed, "Look Ernie! Dad parked the Toyota in the street, and he put my car in the garage! Oh Ernie, that's so sweet!" Naomi jumped from the Volvo and ran to her father, who was standing in the drive-way. "Thanks, Daddy!" Naomi cried, hugging her father.

Felix Martinez laughed. "Beauty rules, baby, and that's a beautiful car."

Ernesto was driving home when he heard a news flash on the radio. A lone robber wearing a hoodie had just hit the twenty-four-seven store. The clerk inside had been shot once in the head.

CHAPTER SEVEN

Ernesto turned numb. The news seemed unreal. The news reporter was saying the condition of the shot clerk was not available. He had been taken away in an ambulance. The robber wore a mask and fired two shots. One went wild, and the other hit the clerk in the head. Witnesses came on the air to describe what they saw.

"It was so terrible," a woman sobbed. "He wore this hideous mask from a movie. The poor clerk went down. I saw the paramedics working on him. He looked bad. I don't think he's gonna make it."

"I never seen nothing so awful," a man said. "He was in and outta the place in a minute. The clerk, he wouldn't hand over the money. He tried to duck behind the counter. The guy vaulted over the counter and shot him. Then he cleaned out the register and ran. I thought I was gonna get shot too."

Ernesto was sick to his stomach. He thought he'd vomit. He pulled over to the curb and hung his head down for a few minutes. His heart was pounding so hard he couldn't count the beats.

Then, slowly, Ernesto pulled out into traffic again. He passed the twenty-four-seven store. Several police cruisers were still there. Yellow crime scene tape hung across the door. The robbery had taken place in broad daylight, just like the robbery at the thrift store. The same robber had probably hit both places.

Ernesto couldn't help thinking about Cruz Lopez. He prayed that Cruz wasn't the gunman who shot the clerk. If he was, Ernesto wouldn't be able to live with himself. He had remained silent when he saw Cruz running down the street after the thrift store was hit.

Ernesto drove home. When he opened the front door, his father met him. "Ernie, you heard about the robbery?" he asked.

"Yeah, I just heard it on the radio," Ernesto replied. His mouth was so dry he could hardly speak.

"Ernie," Dad told him, "your boss at the pizzeria just called—Bashar. He asked me if you could come to work right away. It was Bashar's brother, Amir, who got shot. Amir was the clerk who got shot. Bashar needs to be with the family. They got little kids."

Ernesto had thought he couldn't feel any worse. Now he did. Amir was a brilliant engineering student with a wife and two babies. He went to school but worked two jobs to provide for his family.

Ernesto pulled out his cell phone and called Bashar. "This is Ernie, Bashar," he said. "I'm on my way to the pizzeria. I'll stay as long as I'm needed man. Dad told me what happened. I'm so sorry." Ernesto could hear background sounds that indicated

Bashar was in the emergency room of the hospital.

"Thanks Ernie," Bashar responded in a broken voice. "Amir is bad . . . real bad. He's going into surgery. Pray for us, Ernie."

Ernesto rushed from the house and drove to the pizzeria. Usually, Bashar and Peggy Luna worked at this time on Saturday. Bashar did the deliveries. Peggy never did deliveries. So Ernesto figured the poor girl must be going crazy.

Ernesto parked in the lot and ran in.

"Oh thank God you're here!" Peggy gasped. "I got people calling in orders and screaming at me, Ernie. I didn't know what to do. Bashar flew out of here when he got the call about Amir. You know what happened?" Her eyes were wide and frightened.

"Yeah, his brother got shot," Ernesto said. "Oh man, in daylight again, like the thrift store."

"So many people out of work," Peggy groaned. "I guess they're getting desperate."

125

"Nobody should be that desperate!" Ernesto declared.

Ernesto grabbed a handful of orders and the boxes of pizza. Off he went to make deliveries. Then he sped back to the pizzeria and helped Peggy. For a while, they stuck the pizzas into the oven and took care of the walk-in customers. Ernesto then made two more home deliveries.

After a nightmarish hour, Phil Serra came in a little early for his regular shift. Phil was also a junior at Cesar Chavez High School, and he delivered often.

"Peggy," he said, "where's Bashar? What's Ernie doin' here?"

Peggy just held her hand in the air and replied, "Later, Phil. Not now."

Ernesto breathed a sigh of relief. The pressure was off with Phil on hand. Ernesto and Peggy made the pizzas and took care of the walk-ins. Phil did the deliveries.

Finally, there was a brief lull in business. "Oh man!" Ernesto exclaimed, collapsing on one of the chairs. He had a pounding headache. He'd been so busy for the past couple of hours. He could think of nothing else but keeping the pizzeria going. But now the horrifying fear hit him once more like an ice-cold hand on his heart. Was Cruz the shooter?

"What a horrible thing to have happened to Amir," Peggy remarked when Phil returned from the latest deliveries.

Phil Serra's eyes went wide. Until this moment, he hadn't heard what happened. "What's going on?" he asked. "What happened to Amir?"

"Amir Ghamouri got shot at the twenty-four-seven store," Peggy explained. "That's why Bashar isn't here. He went to the emergency room to be with his brother's family. Bashar got Ernesto to come in. We've been working like crazy."

"Oh my God!" Phil cried, grasping his head. "Amir's such a cool guy. When I go over to the twenty-four-seven store, we always talk math and engineering. He's a math geek like me. He's such a good guy.

He's only about twenty-four, but he's got a wife and those two little kids. Oh my God!" Phil picked up his cell phone and called his girlfriend, Yvette Ozono. He told her what happened.

More customers came into the pizzeria. A few of them had additional information about the robbery.

"My cousin was there when it went down," a young man told them. "He said the robber was a thin guy wearing a hoodie and this horrible mask. The robber was about five seven or eight."

Fresh chills of terror ran up Ernesto's spine. Cruz was thin, about five foot nine.

Ernesto thought he should have done the right thing right after seeing Cruz running that day. He should have tipped off the police then. Maybe none of this horror would be happening. Maybe Amir wouldn't be fighting for his life with a bullet in his head.

If Cruz Lopez was the robber in both crimes, then Ernesto knew he had blood on his hands—Amir's blood. And he didn't think that blood would ever wash off. If Amir didn't make it, Ernesto was sure he couldn't go on. He didn't know what he would do. But everything he loved and dreamed would turn to ashes in his heart and soul.

Ernesto had put his friendship with Paul Morales ahead of his duty as a citizen. If Cruz Lopez had shot Amir, Ernesto could never forgive himself.

The young man was still talking about what his cousin saw at the robbery. "My cousin, he said the robber wore a mask from that movie."

"What movie?" Peggy Luna asked.

"That movie that guy Heath Ledger was in," the man said. "You know, that Batman movie. It was the Joker mask. Yeah, that was it."

"I hope your cousin told the cops about that," Peggy said.

"Yeah, yeah, he did," the young man affirmed.

Ernesto continued working at the pizzeria until eight o'clock. He worked like a robot, going through the motions. All the time, he felt like dying. Bashar had not yet called about his brother's condition. Maybe, Ernesto thought, by now Amir was dead. He was a young, bright family man shot down in his youth. The monster who did it had no respect for human life. Amir was a young man, working on becoming an American citizen. He'd endured horrible conditions in Iraq but had survived them. Now he'd been cut down on a street in the *barrio*.

Two more employees came in at eight. So Ernesto was finally able to leave. He walked out into the dark parking lot. Sitting in his car, he called Abel. "You heard?" he asked.

"Yeah, Bashar's brother got shot," Abel replied. "I went in there all the time, in the twenty-four-seven store. They had good, cheap vegetables."

"Abel," Ernesto said, "what's tearing me apart is that I'm afraid Cruz did it. It's eating me alive, Abel. I should have called the police that day. I should've told them I saw Cruz running away from the thrift store. If only I'd done that, then . . ." Ernesto was almost sobbing.

"The minute I heard what happened, Ernie, I called Paul," Abel told him. "He wasn't answering. I got his voice mail. Then I called the Lopez house. Mr. Lopez said Cruz was gone somewhere. Oh man, Ernie! I feel as bad as you do. If Cruz did this, then I'm guilty too. When you told Paul, you told me too. I could have done the right thing and tipped off the cops. Paul swore us both to secrecy, and we shouldn't have agreed." Abel's voice was filled with remorse.

Ernesto took a deep breath. "Abel, if Cruz did this . . . if he shot Amir, I can't handle it. I mean, I don't know how I can live with myself."

"Take it easy, man," Abel advised. "Don't jump to conclusions. It probably wasn't even Cruz. This guy carried his snake-bit friend across the Anza-Borrego. That's not the kind of guy who'd be low enough to shoot someone in cold blood. We can't be sure. But in my heart I believe he didn't do the crime."

When Ernesto got home, he found his father in the living room working on the computer. Luis Sandoval turned and looked at him. "You look terrible, Ernie," he commented. "Are you all right?"

Ernesto walked over to a chair opposite his father. He sank into the chair and briefly buried his face in his hands. Then he confessed, "Dad, I did a terrible thing."

Ernesto had sworn secrecy to Paul Morales. He promised that he would never tell anyone about seeing Cruz running away that day. But Ernesto had to tell his father now. No matter how awful the consequences might be of not speaking earlier, they could be worse now. If Cruz had robbed twice and shot a man, he could do it again. It was too late for Ernesto to spare himself a terrible, lifelong guilt. But he had to act now to prevent more tragedy.

Luis Sandoval pushed away from the computer. "Talk to me, Ernie."

"Dad, when the thrift store was robbed," Ernesto began. "That day, right after it happened, I saw Cruz Lopez running from the direction of the store. He was running fast, like he was escaping. I told Paul Morales, and he said Cruz never robbed the thrift store. Paul loves Cruz. He loves him like a brother. Paul said if I told the cops, they'd just hassle Cruz even though he's innocent."

Now Ernesto had to admit the worst part of his story. "Paul swore me to secrecy. So I never said anything. I trusted Paul that he knew Cruz well enough to know he didn't rob the thrift store. I trusted Paul, but in my heart I wasn't sure. Now I'm afraid Cruz might have hit the thrift store. And today . . . the twenty-four-seven store too. And I'm worried sick that he . . . he . . . shot Amir."

Ernesto hung his head low. "Dad, don't you see? I could have saved Amir, but I didn't. I kept quiet. I didn't tell the police. Now maybe Amir will die, and it's my fault. It's almost like I killed him." Ernesto was crying.

Luis Sandoval got up and sat beside his son, putting his arms around him. "Take it easy, boy," he said gently.

"Dad," Ernesto sobbed, "I didn't want to make trouble for an innocent person. I know the police hassle Cruz and Beto a lot because of how they look. The Lopez family had enough trouble without me fingering Cruz. His dad is out of work, his mom's sick. I didn't want to make more trouble for them when they were having such a struggle. But I should have called the police. The thrift store robber wore a hoodie, and so did Cruz. He was running. He looked guilty."

"Well, Ernie," Mr. Sandoval responded softly, "I'm not going to mince words. Yes, you needed to have tipped the police off. That would have been the right thing to do.

They would have questioned Cruz. If he didn't do anything, that would have been the end of it. But you took the matter into your own hands. You decided he must be innocent because Paul said so. You put a great deal of faith in Paul's judgment. You put your friendship for Paul ahead of your own conscience."

"Dad," Ernesto moaned, "what do I do now?"

Luis Sandoval closed his eyes for a moment. He pressed his fingertips against the closed lids. Then he spoke. "I have my friend at the police station, Ernie. He's a very good guy. I am calling him right now. He's not on duty, but I have a home number. I'm going to tell him what you saw the day the thrift store was robbed. The robber wore a hoodie, and so did Cruz Lopez. But that's the only connection there is. That and the fact that he was running. My friend will investigate. Don't worry, Ernesto. They're not going blazing up to the Lopez house with a fleet of police cars. Cruz will be questioned. If it looks like he did something wrong, he'll be arrested.

Mr. Sandoval looked at the down-turned head of his son. "We have to do this Ernie, and do it now. God forbid, if Cruz is guilty of shooting Amir, then he's dangerous. He will do it again, and other innocent people will suffer." Dad picked up his phone.

"Yeah Dad," Ernesto admitted. "I'm so sorry. I blew it bad. I'm really sorry."

At ten o'clock Ernesto got a call from Bashar. His brother had survived the surgery, and they were able to remove the bullet. He was now in intensive care. No one could give an accurate prognosis for twenty-four hours. His life still hung in the balance. There was also a chance that, even if he lived, he would be disabled.

Ernesto didn't sleep that night. He lay in the darkness, feeling frightened and guilty. He kept second-guessing himself. Why didn't he do his duty? Why did he keep quiet?

Ernesto wondered what might have happened at the Lopez house tonight? Surely the police had gotten there. Were they taking Cruz into custody? The police were already suspicious of guys with shaved heads who wore baggy clothes. Had they already charged Cruz of the crimes? Did they find a gun? And what about Paul Morales? Had he returned home to find his friend under arrest? By now Paul had probably guessed that Ernesto had blown the whistle. He knew Ernesto had broken his vow. If Cruz Lopez turned out to be innocent, then Paul Morales would probably never forgive Ernesto. But Ernesto didn't care about that tonight. All he prayed for was for Amir to survive in good health and for Cruz to be innocent.

Ernesto had never experienced a longer night. As soon as the night sky lightened, he got up. He went to the kitchen and made himself coffee. He sat at the kitchen table, sick at heart.

He looked at his cell phone. It was about six in the morning. If only, he thought, he could call somebody. He needed to hear something that would make him feel better. Finally, in desperation, Ernesto called the Lopez house. He hated to bother those poor people. But he had to know whether Cruz had been arrested. If he had been, then the cops had probably found the gun, and the nightmare was over.

The phone rang a few times. Ernesto could hardly breathe. Then he heard a voice. A sleepy Cruz Lopez cursed and demanded, "Who's this?"

"Cruz, you okay?" Ernesto asked.

"Man, who's callin' me now?" Cruz snarled. "Ain't it bad enough the cops come to hassle me for nothin' again?"

Ernesto didn't have the courage to identify himself. He disconnected the call. He took a huge gulp of coffee. He closed his eyes and thanked God. For the first time since he had heard about the shooting, he felt the terrible dark cloud lifting. He thought it was possible to hope again.

Ernesto poured more coffee. Then he lay his head on the table. In a few minutes he felt a hand on his back. Ernesto looked up. He saw his father smiling at him. "Is there enough coffee for the both of us?" he asked.

"Dad," Ernesto whispered, "I think it's okay."

"My buddy at the police station just called. It wasn't Cruz," Luis Sandoval reported.

Tears streamed unchecked down Ernesto's face.

At school on Monday, Ernesto walked grimly to class. He was almost afraid of seeing Carmen Ibarra. If she'd been in touch with Paul Morales, she'd know that Ernesto had broken his vow of silence on Cruz.

When Ernesto saw Carmen, he searched her face anxiously. She looked very serious. Ernesto walked toward her. He asked, "You hear that my boss's brother, Amir, got shot, didn't you?"

"Yeah, Yvette told me," Carmen replied. "That's awful. Yvette's boyfriend, Phil Serra, knows Amir real well."

"Carmen, you been in touch with Paul?" Ernesto asked her nervously.

"No," Carmen responded. "He had to go to an electronics convention in LA for his boss. He should be back today."

Abel came along then, and Ernesto asked him, "You hear anything about Cruz?"

"Yeah," Abel answered. "Some cops came to his house. They wanted to talk to Cruz. He was ticked off. He said he didn't do anything. The cops tore up his room, looking for a gun. Somebody said he had a gun or something but they didn't find anything."

Ernesto started to breathe easier. Abel went on. "Cruz said the older cop was pretty cool. He told Cruz they were talking to a lot of guys in the *barrio*, not just him. They weren't hassling just him. They asked where Cruz was when the twenty-four-seven store was hit and the guy got shot.

Turns out Cruz was at a clinic. He had a sore on his foot that festered while he was in the ravine. So they treated it for him. So he had an alibi. Problem solved."

Carmen commented, "I wish Paul didn't have such weird friends. But I guess that's how he is."

Ernesto was relieved. He and Abel exchanged knowing glances. They were both thinking the same thing—"Thank goodness!" It seemed like Luis Sandoval's police friend had given Dad the right information. Cruz was in the clear.

CHAPTER EIGHT

At lunchtime at school, Ernesto's cell phone rang. It was Paul calling, and he sounded pretty upset. "Ernie, I just got back from LA. It looks like it hit the fan in the *barrio* while I was gone. I just got off the phone with Cruz. He said the cops were over there last night questioning him. They were looking for a gun, but Cruz has no gun. What 'bout the shooting, Ernie? What happened?"

"My boss at the pizzeria, Bashar," Ernesto explained. "His brother works over at twenty-four-seven. He got robbed and shot. The robber was wearing a hoodie and a mask. He sounds just like the dude who took down the thrift store. Amir got shot in the head. They operated. He's still alive, but it's touch and go."

"Oh man!" Paul groaned. "At first, I thought Cruz was hanging around the streets when it happened. Why doesn't he just stay home? I told that dude over and over not to be hangin' on the street like that. He'd be stuck with no alibi except for dumb luck."

"Paul," Ernesto interrupted, "Cruz has an alibi. His foot was bothering him since he got outta the ravine. He went into one of those clinics and got it looked at. That was right about the time the shooting took place. He's clean."

"Yeah, he told me that. Thank God, man," Paul responded. "I guess the cops are satisfied then. Oh man, if Cruz got busted for robbery and attempted murder ... I mean, I know the guy and he wouldn't shoot somebody ... but when I heard all that happened. I almost lost it."

Paul Morales always sounded confident. Now his voice was shaky. His usual brash armor was dented.

Ernesto heard doubt in Paul's voice. Paul loved and trusted Cruz as a friend. But just for a few minutes, Paul Morales had wondered whether maybe Cruz *was* involved. "You know what man?" Paul said. "I trust this guy. I'd trust him with my life. He saved my life, and yet I almost cracked. I thought, 'Could the dude have done this? Could he have shot the guy in a moment of panic?' This Amir, he's a young guy, not much older than us. Abel said he's got a wife and two babies. And maybe he's done for. That rocked me, man. I thought, 'What if he did this—*what if Cruz did this*?' Then in a way it was my fault too. You saw him running down the street after the thrift store got hit. You didn't say anything. You told me about it. I told you not to tell anybody, and you didn't. And then this happens."

Paul was quiet for a moment. "Ernie, I put this on you. I kept you from tipping the cops off. I thought, what if this Amir guy dies? What if he ends up a vegetable in a hospital bed connected to tubes the rest of his life. If Cruz was the shooter, I could have prevented that from happening."

Ernesto never thought Paul Morales could be so emotional. Paul was so tough, so brash. But Ernesto had kept quiet about Cruz. And for a short while he thought he might have caused the severe injury or death of another man. Paul seemed to be close to his breaking point.

As Paul and Ernesto talked, Yvette Ozono came along. She'd heard Ernesto mention Paul's name over the phone. She asked, "Is that Paul Morales you're talking to, Ernie?"

"Yeah," Ernesto replied. He told Paul that Yvette had come along.

"Can I talk to him?" Yvette asked.

Yvette had a soft spot in her heart for Paul Morales. Once she was feeling really down. Phil Serra had asked her out, but she felt she wasn't good enough for him. Paul had given her a pep talk that restored her spirits. He'd convinced her that she was a good and valuable person. He'd told her that she should accept Phil's invitation to date her. Ever since then, Yvette and Phil were together a lot.

Ernesto handed Yvette his phone. "Hey Paul," Yvette said, "you know my boyfriend, Phil Serra, who works at the pizzeria with Ernie? Well, the night after Amir was shot, a lotta guys were coming in the pizzeria. A couple of them were witnesses. They were in the twenty-four-seven store when the robber came in. Phil heard one of the guys say the shooter was wearing a mask from that Batman movie. He was the Joker. It was the real scary face that Heath Ledger had in the movie."

Ernesto wondered where Yvette was going with all this. "Well," she went on, "remember when I was hanging with that monster Coyote? He had a friend who liked to wear that Joker mask. Maybe it doesn't mean anything. But this was a real mean sadistic guy, and he loved that joker mask. I was just thinking maybe he's the one who did the two robberies and shot Amir."

"Who is this guy, Yvette?" Paul asked. "Do you know his name?"

"No," Yvette answered, "but he had this crazy laugh. They called him Hyena. Maybe it doesn't even mean anything. I'd feel foolish calling the cops and telling them. Hyena hung out with Coyote and those creeps. One time he pushed me in a closet and locked the door. He told me there was a poisonous snake in there. I almost died of a heart attack. I heard him outside with that crazy laugh. There was no snake, but that's the kind of stuff he did."

"Thanks Yvette. I'll ask around. I know a lot of guys with street cred," Paul said.

Within a few hours Paul Morales had identified Hyena as Mike Soriano. He had a long rap sheet for drugs and assault. He was strung out on heroin and crack cocaine. He lived with his girlfriend in an apartment on Starling. He was almost thirty, but he looked younger.

When the school day was over, Ernesto was jogging home. Paul's pickup came up alongside him. Paul pulled it over to the curb and got out.

"What's up?" Ernesto asked.

On the phone, Paul Morales had sounded like a guy who'd been scheduled to be hanged at noon. Now he looked as though he'd gotten a sudden reprieve and a million dollars to boot. Paul grabbed Ernesto and gave him a hug. "Dude, life is good," he cried. "Bless that little girl, Yvette. She gave us what we needed. With the help of my homies, I ID'd Hyena and called the cops. They went to Soriano's apartment. They found the gun and money from the twenty-four-seven store. It was the gun that was used to shoot Amir. Ernie, listen, when you see Yvette, you give her this, okay?"

Ernesto looked at the crisp hundred dollar bill. His eyes bugged out. "You sure?" he asked.

"Give it to her, man," Paul insisted. "What if she hadn't remembered that monster wearing a joker mask. It might have taken weeks or months to get Soriano. By that time he mighta shot a few more poor chumps tryin' to make a living."

Then the smile left Paul Morales' face. He looked dead serious. "Ernie, you thought it might be Cruz, didn't you?"

Ernesto nodded. "It crossed my mind, man, yeah," he admitted.

Paul took a long breath. "Me too. All I heard was that the twenty-four-seven store was hit, and that it went down just like at the thrift store. That tore me up. I thought maybe Cruz got really desperate with his family going down for the count. Maybe he went in there, Amir gave him a bad time, and it just happened. I didn't want to think Cruz could do something like that, but . . ." Paul's voice trailed off.

"Yeah," Ernesto said.

"You know, man, by telling you not to tip the cops, I screwed you over, dude," Paul admitted. "I was way outta line. I had no right to ask that of you."

Ernesto felt that he had betrayed Paul by telling his father about seeing Cruz. He knew he had to do it, but he felt bad.

"Paul," he confessed, "I kept the secret as long as I could, until Amir got hit. I couldn't keep it after that. I told my dad. If Cruz was guilty, then I had blood on my hands already. I couldn't let it happen again because of me. I just want you to know. I kept the secret as long as I could." He searched the other young man's face, looking for anger, disappointment, any kind of reaction. But Ernesto had to let Paul know the truth.

Paul took a second to react. "You did the right thing, man. No hard feelings. It was my bad that I even asked you to keep quiet." He gave Ernesto another hug.

Ernesto found Yvette and gave her Paul's gift. She looked like she might faint. "Oh wow," she gasped. "I didn't even do anything."

"Chica," Ernesto objected, "you did *everything*."

Ernesto and Naomi drove down to the hospital after school. They had just enough time for a visit before going to work. Bashar had called. He said Amir had been moved from the ICU to a regular room. He was doing better than anyone could have expected. Fortunately, the robber was not such a good shot. The bullet had damaged Amir's skull but never penetrated it. Once the doctors had the blood loss and shock under control, Amir was headed for recovery.

"I'm so glad the cops got the guy who shot Amir," Naomi remarked on the drive to the hospital.

"Yeah, thanks to Phil and Yvette," Ernesto explained. "Phil heard the witness mention the Joker mask. When he told Yvette, she remembered some creep who hung with Coyote who wore Joker masks. That little piece of information cracked the case. The cop told Paul that sometimes one small lead is all they need. You know, Naomi, I thought Cruz had maybe done it.

I mean, his family was in bad shape. And Cruz, man, he was acting weird."

"Yeah," Naomi agreed. "Paul's a nice guy. But those friends of his are sorta on the edge. Boy, that shooting really upset my parents. Dad was almost demanding that I quit Chill Out. It was bad enough when old Mr. Ancho tried to kidnap me, but now these robberies. Dad was going on and on about how precious I was. If something happened to me, he wouldn't want to live anymore. He made me feel horrible. But now that the guy is caught, Dad's cooled down a little. Thank God."

"Yeah," Ernesto said. "Mom asked me if maybe I should quit the pizzeria until the robber was caught. But I love my job, and I really love the money. It makes me feel good to be making my own money. Plus, I couldn't do that to Bashar. We're almost seventeen, Naomi. We can't just let our moms and dads watch over us all the time."

They pulled into the parking garage of the large hospital. They checked in with woman at the information desk. She told them Amir was in room 428 on the fourth floor. Doctors, nurses, and visitors passed them in the corridor.

"There it is," Naomi pointed.

They poked their heads in the door. There sat a pretty young woman with a toddler at her knees. Ernesto assumed she was Amir Ghamouri's wife with one of their kids. Amir's head was bandaged. But he was sitting up in bed and looking good.

"Hello," Ernesto said. "I work for Bashar at the pizzeria. This is my girlfriend, Naomi Martinez."

The woman smiled and nodded. "Bashar said you were so good that night rushing to the pizzeria. Thank you," she said.

Amir grinned at Ernesto and said, "Bashar is always talking about you, Ernesto. He cannot say enough good things about you. You're his right-hand man."

"Bashar is a great guy to work for," Ernesto responded. "The best. So, how are you doing, Amir?"

Amir's head was wrapped in surgical dressing. He had a tube running from his forearm and wires attached to his chest under the hospital gown. A monitor on a floor stand behind him beeped every now and then. He was breathing oxygen from a clear tube clamped to his nose. Ernesto thought he looked sleepy—probably because of painkiller medicine. But Amir was fairly chipper. He looked as though he'd be okay.

"The doctors say I am doing much better than they thought I would. It looks like I'm gonna be okay, praise God. They're talking about kicking me outta here pretty soon," Amir replied, laughing.

"Great," Ernesto said. "We're all pulling for you, man. I don't know if you heard or not. They caught the guy who shot you."

"Bashar told me," Amir said. "I was so glad."

"You know, Amir," Ernesto explained, "your friend Phil Serra came up with the key lead. He and his girlfriend had the clue that helped the cops catch the shooter. Phil heard somebody say the robber wore a Joker mask. Yvette remembered some monster from her past who wore Joker masks all the time. Turns out that's all the cops needed."

"If you see him before I do, please thank him and Yvette for me," Amir said. "Phil's a good friend. We both love mathematics. Sometimes we talk about starting some high-tech business together. Developing the next big thing."

Bashar and his wife arrived for their visit then. Bashar hugged Ernesto. "This is my top guy at the pizzeria," Bashar declared.

"Bashar," Ernesto told him, "I'll do any extra shifts you need at the pizzeria. I'll come every afternoon and nights too if you need me. I want you to feel free to help Amir and his family until he's back on his feet."

Bashar put his arm around Ernesto's shoulders. "You hear this kid? Is this a wonderful kid? If my own kids should grow up like this, I will get on my knees and thank the Lord." Bashar turned to Naomi. "This is your boyfriend, eh?"

"Yes," Naomi answered, smiling.

"Keep him," Bashar commanded. "Keep him, little girl. They do not make many like this. Don't let him go."

"Oh, I don't intend to," Naomi said, laughing.

When they left the hospital parking structure, Ernesto checked his watch. They had some time before they had to go to work. "Naomi," Ernesto announced, "I'm hungry. I could eat the steering wheel if it had some mustard on it. I gotta stop for something. A hamburger, I think. Yeah, that's what I need right now."

Ernesto pulled into the first hamburger stand he saw. He felt having like the biggest hamburger on the menu. He wanted onions, lettuce, tomatoes, pickles, and cheese. He wanted it slathered with a rich dressing that oozed out the sides of the bun. Ernesto wanted a burger too big to get his mouth around. And he wanted a mound of French fries and onion rings on the side. To wash it down, he wanted a jumbo cola with lots of ice.

Before Cruz was cleared, Ernesto not only couldn't sleep, but he had stopped eating. Now the terrible fear and guilt were lifted from his shoulders. Suddenly, he was starving.

Ernesto's hamburger deluxe was delivered to the table. Naomi looked at the dish and then gave her small salad a dirty look. "Oh boy, Ernie, your burger looks so good," she commented.

"Yep," was all he said. She stared at the hamburger in Ernesto's hands. Then jumped up, rushed to the counter, and ordered the same dish for herself.

Back at the table, Naomi took a bite of her burger. "Oh, this is so delicious. It's been ages since I had a hamburger this good. It doesn't say on the wrapper here how many calories it is. What do you think?"

"Oh, maybe six thousand," Ernesto replied with a wicked grin.

"No!" Naomi protested. "Not six thousand! That's impossible." A piece of paper in the tray listed the calories for the menu items. Naomi took another big bite of her burger and poked a couple of fries into her mouth. As she munched, she picked up the paper and looked for their hamburger dishes on it. "Let's see, our hamburger is called 'The Jumbo-Jumbo Kitchen Sink.' " She traced the line across the paper with her finger. "*Ay no!*" she exclaimed. "Ernie! With the double burger, all the dressings, the French fries and onion rings, and the supersized cola, that's twenty-five hundred calories! That's five hundred calories more than a person is normally supposed to eat all day!"

"I'm not normal," Ernesto said. He sank his teeth into what was left of the juicy burger. He was ignoring the dressing dribbling on his chin. "I don't care. Right now I don't care. I haven't eaten hardly anything for three days. I deserve this. I'm a growing boy. I'll jog to and from school all next week." He continued to cram the hamburger down. He lubricated the way into his stomach with gulps of soda.

Naomi started to laugh. She pulled out her phone and took a picture of Ernesto eating his hamburger.

Ernesto paused in his eating. He stared at Naomi. "Babe," he asked, "you didn't just take a picture of me, did you? You didn't take a picture of me gorging myself on this burger. Did you?"

Naomi laughed harder. "Of course I did. You looked so cute. It's going on Facebook. Or maybe I'll just save it. Years from now, we'll be living in our little house somewhere, and we'll have our first fight. Then I'll blackmail you with it. I'll threaten to use the picture on our Christmas cards."

"Don't you dare," Ernesto said, finally wiping his chin. He popped the last few fries into his mouth. "Oh man, that was the best hamburger I have ever had in my entire life. Maybe being so hungry made it taste so incredible. Boy, I needed that. I can just feel the life returning to my body."

They finished their colas and walked outside to Ernesto's Volvo.

Ernesto was going to drop Naomi at Chill Out and then drive over to the pizzeria. They had just enough time to get to work.

"You know, babe," Ernesto said, "I not only haven't been eating. I haven't been sleeping either. I just tossed and turned all night worrying that maybe Cruz Lopez had shot Amir."

"Ernie, I was concerned too," Naomi replied. "But why were you so upset about it There's nothing you could do about it."

"Babe, there was something I could do," Ernesto confessed. He told her about seeing Cruz running away from the thrift store right after the holdup. He told her about Paul telling him not to tell the cops.

"I was so ashamed," Ernesto confessed. "I felt like a criminal myself. I thought I had information that might help the police stop a robber and I wasn't telling them. I felt like I was—what do they call it?—abetting a crime. It was so weird. You never think you'll act a certain way until suddenly you do. But now I'll sleep like a baby. Tomorrow morning mom will have to pry me out of bed with a crowbar. Even that might not work."

"I wish you would have come to me, Ernie," Naomi scolded him gently. "That's a time when I should be by your side."

Ernesto nodded his head and looked very sad. Naomi knew she'd made him feel worse about his behavior.

"Okay!" she declared, trying to sound as cheerful as she could. "Now all we have to worry about is getting you elected senior class president. The election is just two weeks away. You better be writing a good speech telling the kids why you'd be best for the job. I bet you haven't even started that."

"You're right, Naomi," Ernesto admitted. "I was so upset about what happened to Amir that I couldn't think of anything else. I even flunked a pop quiz in history. Thank heaven I don't have Dad for a teacher! My poor history teacher is used to me getting all As. Then I totally flunk some stupid little quiz."

"Well, get busy on your speech, Ernie," Naomi commanded, snuggling against him.

"Yeah," Ernesto declared in a mocking tone. "The first speech of my political career. Someday they'll show it on TV. 'Here's President Ernesto Sandoval when he was just sixteen years old and running for senior class president.' "

CHAPTER NINE

At Chavez High School the next day, Naomi Martinez pulled up in her gold Chevy classic. She was instantly surrounded by admiring friends.

"Ohhh, it's beautiful, Naomi!" Carmen Ibarra cried.

"Gorgeous!" Yvette Ozono exclaimed.

Another girl, Gloria Navarez, stood at the edge of the excited, giggling crowd. She looked at Naomi and asked, "That guy running for senior class president—Sandoval. He's your boyfriend, isn't he?"

Naomi had seen Gloria in several of her classes, but they weren't friends. Gloria had the reputation of being a gossip. "Yeah, why?" Naomi asked.

"I heard," Gloria replied, "that his family had to leave Los Angeles 'cause he was in a lot of trouble there. He had a really bad rep."

"That's not true," Naomi objected. "They cut back on teachers in Ernie's father's school district. Mr. Sandoval got a new job here at Chavez. That's why the family moved."

"That's not what I heard," Gloria insisted. "How do you know what he's told you is true? You just met him a few months ago. None of us really know him." Gloria edged a little closer. "I heard he was really wild up there. He was drinking and driving, getting DUIs, and using drugs too."

Carmen Ibarra looked angry. "Where did you hear all this?" she demanded, "I never heard such garbage in my life."

"It's all over the school," Gloria replied. "Everybody's talking about it. All the bad stuff about Ernesto Sandoval was kept hidden 'cause his uncle is a lawyer and stuff.

He erased the records or something, and the family came down here . . ."

"Gloria," Yvette Ozono told her, "you shouldn't be spreading nasty rumors like that. Especially since they're not true." She turned to Naomi. "I got a good idea where these rumors got started, I heard that creep, Clay Aguirre, yesterday. He was saying stuff like this at the vending machine."

"Well," Gloria insisted, "all I know is, we don't want a guy like that for senior class president. My dad always says, 'Where there's smoke, there's fire.' Why should we elect somebody we don't hardly know? The other two who're running have been at Chavez since ninth grade. Before that, we knew them in middle school. Sandoval is a stranger."

Another girl who was standing nearby looked thoughtful. "Yeah, that's sort of true," she agreed. "A lot of us don't know Ernesto Sandoval that well. He came just at the beginning of junior year. I've known Mira Nuñez since fourth grade."

Carmen Ibarra shook her head bitterly. "It looks like the dirty rumor machine is working again. That's just like it was when my dad was running for city council, Naomi. Remember when all those slanderous flyers suddenly appeared filled with lies about my dad?"

"Yeah, but smears like that don't work," Naomi declared. "People see through them."

Ernesto parked his Volvo beside Naomi's gold car, got out, and whistled. "Oh man, I hope my poor old Volvo doesn't get an inferiority complex sitting here."

Another boy looked at Ernesto Sandoval and asked, "Hey, Sandoval, did you get into a jam up in LA? They're saying you and your folks had to leave there. You were busted for DUIs and drugs."

Ernesto was surprised. He felt a little angry. But he said calmly, "No, I never had any DUIs in LA. I was a fifteen-year-old sophomore. I wasn't even driving yet. I got my driver's license down here. Where did you hear that?"

"It's all over the school," the boy said.

"Well, it's a lie," Ernesto asserted. "The drug thing is a lie too. The only drug I do is an aspirin when I got a headache."

When Ernesto was alone with Naomi, he asked, "What's going on? Overnight I've turned into a drunken drug user with a dark past."

"Somebody started the rumors, Ernie," Naomi answered. "Like they did against Carmen's dad when he ran for city council. It's easy to get slanderous rumors started. Like cutting open a feather pillow on a windy day. Pretty soon the feathers are everywhere. Carmen heard Clay Aguirre talking trash about you. So that's probably where it all got going."

"Well," Ernesto said, "nothing much we can do about a whispering campaign."

"Ernie, most of the kids know you as a good guy," Naomi assured him. "They're not going to buy this dirty business. I mean, look, we're two weeks away from the senior class president election. All of a sudden, it comes out that you've done all kinds of bad things. It's so obvious that it's a smear."

A little later, Ernesto was walking toward Ms. Hunt's English class. Abel Ruiz came up alongside him. "Ernie, two guys just asked me if I knew about your drunk driving arrests in Los Angeles," he said. "I told the fools you were only fifteen years old and you couldn't even drive. I asked them where they got that. They said some guy is talking about it. I figure we can guess who the guy is."

Ernesto shrugged. "People love gossip. They just eat it up. Like with the celebrities. You look at those stupid tabloids. Some actor or actress has given a million dollars to charity, and it's buried on the last page. But the headlines on the front of the rags are screaming about some scandal. I guess people like to tear other people down because then it makes them feel bigger. They think they're not so bad after all if someone else is doing worse stuff."

"I hate gossip," Abel declared. "It's like a cowardly thing to do. I guess Aguirre really wants Mira to win the election. It's not that he cares that much for her. He just wants to stick it to you. Sometimes, Ernie, I sorta feel sorry for Clay Aguirre."

Ernesto turned. "Feel *sorry* for him?" he asked in surprise.

"Yeah," Abel said. "It must be horrible to be him. It must make him retch to wake up every morning in that mean body."

Both boys laughed.

When Ernesto walked into English class, he noticed Ms. Hunt staring at him in a strange way. For a minute, Ernesto was afraid she had heard the rumors and wondered whether they might be true. She really liked and respected Ernesto. He knew she would feel terrible if he was hiding a dark past.

Ernesto liked Ms. Hunt too. She was his favorite teacher. He would really be disappointed if she bought any of that slander. Surely, he thought, someone as intelligent as Ms. Hunt would see what was happening. But she *was* looking at Ernesto today in a different way.

"Today we will continue with the short stories we are studying," the teacher announced. "But first we're going to do something a little different. Since the senior class elections are coming up, I think we're going to call on Shakespeare to clarify what an election is all about. Specifically, we will be going to *Othello*. You all remember when we tackled *Othello* before." Ms. Hunt smiled. "Shakespeare's plays were written hundreds of years ago, but they are relevant today. That's the timelessness of great literature. For every generation, the truth of these plays shines light on our own lives."

Ms. Hunt went to the whiteboard, which showed a quote from *Othello*. "I'm sure you all remember this quote," Ms. Hunt remarked. "It's one of the most memorable from *Othello*. I'm going to ask one of our students to read this quote and then tell us what it means. Let's choose someone with a very strong voice. That kind of voice is appropriate to reading a line from Shakespeare."

Ms. Hunt glanced around the room as if she were looking for just the right student. But she seemed to already know whom she was going to choose. She smiled at Clay Aguirre and directed, "Clay, would you read the quote please? And then tell us in your own words what it means to you."

Clay Aguirre looked shocked. He never expected to be called upon. Clay shifted uncomfortably in his seat. He looked at Ms. Hunt, cleared his throat, and stared at the quote.

"You can start anytime, Clay," Ms. Hunt said. She was smiling very sweetly. She didn't usually smile quite so sweetly. Ernesto sensed an ulterior motive in her smile.

"Uh . . ." Clay began. "'Good name in man and woman, dear my lord, is the immediate jewel of their souls. Who steals my purse steals trash. 'Tis something, nothing:

171

'Twas mine, 'tis his, and has been slave to thousands: But he that filches from me my good name . . . .'" Clay coughed. He shifted uncomfortably again in his seat. He cleared his throat.

"Clay, please begin again with 'but he that filches.' Continue from there to finish the quote," Ms. Hunt said.

"'But he that filches from me my good name,'" Clay said, "'robs me of that which not enriches him and makes me poor indeed.'"

"Excellent reading of the quote, Clay," Ms. Hunt commended him. "Could you tell us now what it meant to you?"

"Uh . . . well," Clay stammered. "It means if you say bad things about people, you know, spread stuff that's not so . . . it like does a lot of harm. It's sorta worse than stealing somebody's money."

"Exactly, Clay," Ms. Hunt responded. "Well done. So, class, do you see how relevant the quote is to a political campaign? It applies even to one as small as our senior class elections. Sometimes, in major elections, candidates are so desperate to win that they slander their opponents. The same can happen right here at Cesar Chavez High if we let it. If a student is so eager to win, or to see a friend win, he might resort to saying nasty things about opponents."

A girl raised her hand. Ms. Hunt nodded toward her. "Last year in the governor's race, one of the candidates put out an ad," the girl said. "It hinted that his opponent had misused funds. It wasn't true. But the accused candidate got covered with a lot of mud."

"And that wasn't fair, was it?" Ms. Hunt asked.

"Sometimes candidates put out these attack ads," another boy added. "They say really bad things about their opponents, things that are so not true. And then a lot of people who aren't so smart just believe everything. That stuff makes me mad."

"I think it makes us all angry when something like that happens," Ms. Hunt responded. "In a fair campaign, the candidates tell why they feel they are the best. But slander and smears are never acceptable. They are not acceptable in national races. And they are not acceptable here on our campus."

Carmen Ibarra raised her hand. "When my dad ran for city council, somebody printed flyers filled with lies about him. The flyers were spread all over the school and in the neighborhood too. They accused my father of being some kind of a criminal. It was all lies but it hurt a lot."

Ms. Hunt nodded. "Yes, I remember that, Carmen. It was very disturbing. So now, what can we do if someone starts a rumor? Suppose someone comes up to us on campus." The teacher dropped her voice to a stage whisper. "'Psst, you know that Buzzie Chuzzlewit who's running for senior class president? He's actually an invading alien from a distant planet!'"

Laughter broke out in the classroom. But Clay Aguirre wasn't laughing.

"I'll ask that person how he knows that," Yvette Ozono said. "I'll demand proof that Buzzie is really an alien from another planet."

More laughter from the class.

"I'll tell that person that she's got no business spreading rumors," a boy added.

"I'll just laugh and tell the gossip to go stuff a banana in his mouth," another student said.

Ms. Hunt laughed too. "So that concludes our little exercise," she summed up. "Listen carefully to the candidates when they make their speeches and ask for your vote. Read their posters, and talk to them if you can. Base your voting decision on your personal inquiries. We need to be well informed, and we need to be fair. You might meet someone who is conducting a smear campaign against one of our students. You need to remind that person that we are all Americans in the greatest nation on earth. And we *play fair*."

The class applauded Ms. Hunt. Then she returned to the unit on short stories.

Clay Aguirre had slumped in his chair.

As the students filed out, Clay Aguirre asked Mira Nuñez, "What was that all about in the first part of class? It sounds like Ms. Hunt went a little nuts. Was that weird or something?"

Mira Nuñez said nothing.

Ernesto left class with Naomi. What Ms. Hunt had done deeply touched him. Apparently, she was responding to the rumors against Ernesto that were sweeping the school. She understood what was happening. She dealt with the gossip in a smooth, professional way without pointing the finger of suspicion at anyone.

"Naomi," Ernesto asked, "did that just happen? Or was I dreaming?"

Naomi grinned. "Is she cool or what?" she remarked.

When Ernesto went to lunch with Abel Ruiz, Julio, Dom, and Carlos, he was still hearing murmurs about his troubled past.

But there were a lot fewer of them than in the morning. Fewer students were spreading the lies.

Ernesto made sure to bring one of Mom's sandwiches with him today. He lay on the grass eating it. Sometimes she made a traditional Mexican *torta* on a *bolillo*. But today the theme was Irish. The corned beef sandwich had really good mustard, and the rye bread was chewy and tasty. Ernesto had intended to wash it down with that healthy vegetable juice. But, again, he ended up with his orangey carbonated drink. He told himself that next week he would surely go for the vegetable juice.

He was staring up at the big puffy clouds in the sky. It had rained yesterday. Though now the sun was shining, the clouds lingered. Occasionally one blocked the sun and created a momentary darkness. Ernesto was so contented at the moment that he didn't even notice the shadow fall across his face.

"Hi Ernie," Naomi said. "Is this a strictly guys only lunch spot? Or can a girl sit down here too?"

"Depends on the girl," Ernesto answered, grinning. "In this case, babe, you are more than welcome."

Naomi sat down. "Ernie, and the rest of you guys too," she announced, "you have to catch the six thirty local news tonight on Channel 8. There's a real cute story on, and you can't miss it. It's an animal story."

"Oh wow," Julio said. "Heart be still! There's a little baby orphan squirrel that has been adopted by a kitty cat. Oh man, I gotta write that down. I can't miss it."

"Nah," Dom Reynosa clowned. "I bet it's a story about a trained poodle that plays Beethoven on the piano."

"Or hey," Carlos joined in. "Maybe a bunny rabbit learned to use the kitty litter box. Don't want to miss that, dudes."

"All right, you guys," Naomi said. "Make fun of it. But you gotta watch Channel 8 at six thirty."

"What's the deal, babe?" Ernesto asked, finishing his lunch with a huge gulp of sticky sweet orange pop.

"All I can say, Ernie," Naomi insisted, "is that, if you don't watch it, I will never forgive you."

"Whoa!" Julio exclaimed. "That's heavy, man. The chick's bringing out the big guns. Clear your schedule, dude. This chick means business."

"Now I'm curious enough to watch it too," Dom chimed in. "But if it does turn out to be a poodle playing the piano, I'm gonna be ticked off."

"You'll watch it. Right, Ernie?" Naomi asked grimly.

"Right," Ernesto confirmed. "I'm brave, but not brave enough to cross you on this, Naomi."

"Good," Naomi said, getting up. She looked at Ernesto's orange drink. "Remember, next week, vegetable juice."

When Ernesto got out of school and turned his cell phone on, he found a message from Bashar. Amir had made even more improvement. They were planning to bring him home in the next few days. Ernesto was happy about that. He thought Bashar was going to call him for an extra shift. Then he would miss the six thirty local news. He'd had enough trauma in his life lately. He didn't want to face Naomi tomorrow and tell her he'd missed the show.

At dinner, Ernesto's parents, *Abuela*, and his sisters were all busily eating. He mentioned the rumors about him at school. "When I got there this morning," he said, "it was like I'd turned into a monster overnight. Kids were looking at me like I was weird. It was kinda scary."

"Clay Aguirre I suppose," Dad commented, frowning. "He was behind that smear attack on Mr. Ibarra. Remember Clay trying to sink Ibarra so that Felix Martinez's cousin could keep his job? Clay thought that would get him in good with the Martinez family. Maybe Naomi would go back to him."

Luis Sandoval took a sip of water as he ate. "I don't understand the guy's thinking. It's not only evil, but it's so stupid too. You know, though, I try not to think that some people are really evil. I try to give them the benefit of the doubt. But in Clay's case, my theory is sorely tested."

Ernesto also described what Ms. Hunt had done in English class. "When I walked into class, Ms. Hunt was just looking at me strangely. For a minute I almost freaked. I thought she'd heard the dirty stories and maybe she half believed them."

Ernesto took another helping of *carne asada*. He was still hungry. "But then Ms. Hunt did such a beautiful thing. She knew exactly who was behind the smear campaign. So she gets us to look at a quote from *Othello*. It was about how it's worse to ruin a reputation than it is to steal money. She calls on Clay Aguirre to read it! Clay looked like he'd chewed on a lemon! Anyway, Ms. Hunt gave a wonderful presentation on running a fair election.

It seemed to take the wind right out of the smear."

"That's great, honey," Mom responded. "She's a very special teacher."

Ernesto glanced at the wall clock as they finished dessert. Ernesto ate the last of his slice of cherry pie. "You guys," he announced, "Naomi warned me to watch the six thirty news 'or else.' Okay if I turn on the TV?"

"Oh yes, let's," Mom agreed.

"Naomi said there's a cute animal story on," Ernesto said, grimacing. "Not that I don't like animals but . . ."

"Can me and Juanita go out and play?" Katalina asked.

"No," Mom insisted emphatically. "We all have to gather in the living room to watch the cute animal story. Right Ernie?" Mom smiled in a strange way.

Ernesto stared at his mother. Did she and Naomi know something he didn't know? Ernesto knew his mom loved animals. But how she marched the family into the living room now was eerie.

CHAPTER TEN

The Sandoval family were seated in front of the television set a few minutes before six thirty. At the top of the show, the anchorwoman announced the news items for that night's show. "And right after the weather," she said, "there's a dog story you don't want to miss."

Ernesto groaned. He bet Dom was right. It *was* about a trained poodle playing the piano. Ernesto looked over at his pretty mother. In another few months, she would give birth to her fourth child, a son. His parents had already named him Alfredo. Ernesto had never seen his mother looking so radiant and happy. For that he was very grateful, even if it meant looking at TV pieces about trained poodles playing the piano.

Maybe, Ernesto thought, her pregnancy was affecting her in bizarre ways. Maybe she craved stories about trained poodles. Perhaps her hormones had driven her love of animals to a fever pitch.

Ernesto glanced over at his father. He seemed very content. He didn't seem to mind Mom's demand that the entire family watch TV. Dad was very tolerant of Mom's wishes, especially now that she was expecting another child. He always treated her with love and respect. But since she was expecting the baby, he went overboard. Mom seemed to grow even more precious to him. Luis Sandoval would watch the poodle play the piano if that would please Mom.

Then, at last, the news item came on. One of the feature reporters was standing in a downtown bookstore. "Local author, Maria Sandoval," the reporter began, "is signing copies of her new picture book—*Thunder and Princess*."

Ernesto's jaw dropped. As the reporter spoke, the screen switched to Maria Sandoval, smiling as she signed books.

"It's Mama!" Juanita screamed.

"Shhh," Katalina said sharply, "I wanna hear."

The reporter went on. "There's been a lot of bad publicity about pit bulls. But Sandoval is out to give us another side of the story. To do that, she had the help of her friends, the Martinez family, including pit bull Brutus, the family pet."

The screen switched again. This time, the Martinez family appeared inside the bookstore. Felix Martinez was grinning broadly. Linda Martinez beside him, holding Brutus on a leash. Behind them were Zack and Naomi. Naomi looked stunning.

Now the screen was filled with Mom, the Martinezes, and the reporter. "I based the story of *Thunder and Princess*," she explained, "on the pit bull of my friends, the Martinez, family. His name is Brutus."

185

"I was really afraid of Brutus at first," Linda Martinez added. "I thought all pit bulls were mean and dangerous."

"Yeah," Felix Martinez laughed. "She'd lock herself in the kitchen 'cause she was afraid he'd get her!"

There was a quick shot of Naomi kneeling and rubbing Brutus with both hands.

"But," Naomi said, "we all learned Brutus was a sweet and lovable guy."

"And now he's part of the family," Zack added.

The last scene contained the reporter and Mom. The interviewer smiled and stated, "Maria Sandoval always wanted to be a writer. Now this mother of three, and soon to be mother of four, has launched her exciting writing career. And it is all because of a big white dog named Brutus. The pooch wormed his way into the hearts of a family and a neighborhood, even though he's a pit bull."

Mom finished the piece. "My book is not just about a pit bull. It is about never judging animals or people by their appearance. What is in the heart is more important than what's on the outside. My book is about tolerance and love."

The reporter added his byline, and the show went to commercial.

The Sandoval family sat for a moment in silent shock.

Luis Sandoval was the first to speak. "Didn't she look beautiful? Mom never looked so beautiful."

"Dad, you knew, huh?" Ernesto asked.

"Sort of," Dad admitted. "They did the piece about a week ago. Your mother was so excited. She wanted to surprise you guys. Naomi did too. Naomi looked so lovely too. And Felix Martinez, didn't he look happy? It was so good to see him smiling. Did you notice he put his arm around Linda's shoulders? And Brutus. That big guy really stole the show."

Ernesto's cell phone was ringing. He picked it up. It was Naomi. "Well, did you enjoy the piece about the poodle playing the piano?" she asked.

"Oh babe, it was awesome!" Ernesto exclaimed. "I mean, you looked so good, and Mom looked fabulous."

Maria Sandoval sat in her chair grinning like a Cheshire cat. "We taped it for my mom and dad," she announced. "Mom's gonna really like it, to see her daughter on TV. Mom can show it to all her jealous friends. For a little while she won't feel so bad about me not being a CEO of some big company or something."

The next week was campaign week. When Ernesto came to school that Monday, all the posters for the candidates were up. Ernesto knew he was biased. But he thought that Carmen, Dom, and Carlos had made the best posters by far. They were beautiful and tasteful. Mira Nuñez had some nice posters too. Even Rod Garcia's friends had done a good job, but nobody expected him to win.

The contest for senior class president was really between Ernesto and Mira

Nuñez. It had been that way at the beginning, and now it was more so.

The smear campaign that Clay Aguirre and his friends had launched still had some buzz. Ernesto found one of his posters defaced with the words "DUI druggie." But Carmen quickly repaired the poster and blanked out the slurs.

As Ernesto walked toward his first class, Clay sidled up beside him. "Mira is gonna win, you know," he declared.

"Maybe so," Ernesto replied. "She's a good person."

"She's really popular," Clay added. "Really hot too. Last two senior class presidents have been guys. It's a girl's turn."

"May the best candidate win," Ernesto stated, trying to avoid an argument.

"My girlfriend's gonna be senior class president," Clay gloated. "I'm glad I'm not with Naomi anymore. Mira is way better. You and Naomi are a pair of losers."

Ernesto stopped walking. He turned to face Clay. One of Clay's feet shifted backward slightly, as if to be ready to run. "No more outta you about Naomi, dude. Or I might just forget that fighting isn't allowed on campus. I'm gonna look around and make sure no teacher is watching. Then I'm gonna knock all your front teeth out."

Clay turned pale, turned, and walked away.

Ernesto smiled to himself.

Wednesday was the day the candidates were to make their speeches. When Ernesto woke up that day, he felt queasy. He didn't eat his usual ham-and-egg burrito. He made do with cottage cheese and orange juice. His speech was written and in his binder. But he wouldn't read from it. He had it memorized.

Ernesto had worked hard on his speech. The candidates had been told to keep the speeches brief and positive. Each candidate had five minutes to talk. The order of appearance had been decided by drawing playing cards. The high card went first, low card last. Rod was going first, Mira second, and Ernesto last. Being last had its advantages and disadvantages. Ernesto had more time to worry as the others spoke. But the last speech was often the one people remembered best.

The day was cool and windy as Ernesto arrived on campus. Naomi rode with him to give him moral support.

"Everybody loves you, Ernie," she assured him. She kissed him before she got out of the car.

"Not everybody, but I hope enough to get me in," Ernesto said. He never thought he would want to win as much as he did now. When he first decided to run, he thought it would be okay if he lost. Now he was fired up. Winning meant a lot to him. He wanted to do some things as senior class president. He knew he'd be deeply disappointed if he lost.

The wind was even stronger when the juniors gathered in the bleachers to hear the candidates make their presentations.

The nine students sat at their places behind the podium. They were running not only for senior class president, but also for vice president and secretary-treasurer. As he sat waiting for his turn, the wind whipped Ernesto's longish dark hair. He regretted not getting a haircut a few days ago. He had another raccoon on his head.

The speeches began. The candidates for treasurer assured the students they were good at math and would take good care of the funds. The vice presidential candidates vowed to improve things at Chavez.

Then the candidates for senior presidents gave their speeches. Rod Garcia made a rather bland presentation that focused on what he had done for the environment. It would have been a good speech if he was running for president of the ecology club again. But it didn't make him look or sound like a senior class president. He got lukewarm applause.

Then Mira Nuñez stood up. She looked gorgeous in a yellow sweater. If looks alone made the difference, Ernesto thought she'd win without saying a word.

"I came here to Chavez High as a freshman," Mira began. "Since then, I have loved this school very much. I am so proud of the students here and how they throw their hearts into all kinds of projects."

Mira spent a few minutes speaking about her achievements as junior vice president. She talked about the clubs, the programs, and the teams at the school. She explained what she would like to do to improve them. She came across as intelligent and full of purpose.

She concluded her speech smartly, with a call for action. "The students who participate in all these programs make me proud and happy to be a student at Chavez High. But one thing makes me sad."

Mira glanced over to where Clay Aguirre was sitting. "You all know about our football team, the awesome Cougars. They're having such a great season. We stand a good chance of being in the regional finals for the championship. Well, that makes me sad."

Mira paused to let her audience wonder why a winning team would make her sad. She continued. "A lot of students don't come to the games. The guys are playing their hearts out. And it just breaks my heart to see all those empty seats. Our guys have given us great, exciting football. Yet when I see big gaps in the bleachers, I can't understand the lack of school pride and spirit. We are just not supporting our wonderful football team as much as we should. As senior class president, I'm going to raise the level of Chavez High spirit. I want our athletes to win their championships to the cheers of every student on campus!"

Mira Nuñez got a lot of applause for her speech. Some of the kids stood on their seats and roared their approval. It took quite some time to quell the applause enough for Ernesto to take the podium.

Ernesto Sandoval was more nervous than he expected to be. His legs were always very strong from the many hours he spent jogging. But now they seemed weak and wobbly, like cooked noodles. He knew he had a case of nerves. Ernesto's stomach growled. He should have eaten more than that measly cottage cheese.

Ernesto stood there and looked out at the faces of his fellow students.

"I want to be your senior class president," Ernesto began in a shaky voice, "But before I tell you why, let me tell you more about myself. I cannot expect your vote unless you know more about me."

Ernesto felt strength coming back into his legs. His voice became firmer. The first few words had blown away his butterflies.

He had decided that he had to assure the students about his past. They had to know why his family had moved out of the *barrio* and then back. He spent a few minutes talking about his life before he came to Chavez High. He described his life in Los Angeles, both at home and at school. He did not mention the smear campaign. But he was countering it in a civil way.

"And now," Ernesto stated, "I will tell you why I want to be senior class president. It is because I don't want to lose a single one of you."

Ernesto paused to let the students try to make the connection. The audience was dead quiet. Then he went on.

"A lot of students drop out. And it's easy to forget them. It's easier to focus on the kids who make it to graduation day. But right now I'm thinking about the kid who's falling behind in math so bad that he's giving up. I'm thinking about the kids who just can't keep up. You've seen them. You've heard what they have to say. To them, school is a daily nightmare. Before long, they're skipping classes. Then they're skipping days. Then they just drop out. And the street gets hold of some of them."

The students were listening. Ernesto went on. "I want to start a mentoring program among the seniors. The school already provides tutors for struggling students. But I want this to come from us. I want students to be helping one another. I don't want even one kid to drop out because he or she has no one to turn to. I want our senior class to turn into a *familia* of *hermanas y hermanos*."

Ernesto felt he was gaining momentum with his audience. "But I don't want to stop there. Keeping kids in school is one thing. Bringing dropouts back to school is another. There are kids out there in the *barrio* right now who should be here with us. I want to try to bring them back. I want to organize senior volunteers to reach out into the *barrio* and try to bring them back. On graduation day, I want to look out at our students in caps and gowns. And I want to see friends we've helped. I want to see everybody there."

From the audience, Naomi caught Ernesto's eye. Her hands were together, as if she was praying. Her fingertips were pressed to her lips. She nodded slowly to him. He knew she was telling him he was doing great.

"If I become your senior class president," Ernesto pledged, "I will work for you, for every one of you. This school is named for a great man—Cesar Chavez. *La causa* for him was the welfare of the farm-workers who he raised up. I have *una causa* too. *Mi causa* is you. It's every one of you. I will walk with you because none of us should walk alone. Working together, we can make this happen. *Sí, se puede!* . . . Thank you. And *viva la causa!*"

Out of the corner of his eyes, Ernesto saw Naomi leap to her feet, shouting and clapping. Others jumped to their feet and applauded loudly. The applause was strong and lasted long. But Ernesto wasn't sure they'd vote him in.

With the assembly concluded, Naomi made her way to Ernesto and hugged him. "You were wonderful!" she praised him. "I'm not just saying that. You were inspirational, babe!"

"Thanks," Ernesto replied. He felt numb. He was neither optimistic nor pessimistic. He was just numb.

Thursday was voting day for the senior offices. In the morning homeroom, every junior student received a ballot with the names of all the candidates. Over the course of the day, the students would cast their votes in the auditorium. The school administrators and teachers wanted the experience to be like voting in a regular election. So the students went to small voting booths, marked their ballots, and deposited the ballots in boxes. For each student, the voting began right after the morning homeroom and continued until classes ended in the afternoon. The teachers would count the votes overnight. The results would be announced at the end of school on Friday.

When the PA system came on that Friday afternoon, Ernesto sat rigidly in his seat. He had a moment of deep gloom. He wondered how he could ever have expected any of the students to vote for him—a stranger.

The principal's voice explained that the winners of the senior class election would now be announced. The new secretary was named, then the treasurer, and then the vice president. Without a pause, the principal moved quickly on.

"For senior class president," the principal's voice stated, "Ernesto Sandoval."

Ernesto didn't know all the students in math class. But they crowded around him, slapping him on the back and high-fiving him. Ernesto's world was spinning, and the faces blurred before him. Outside the classroom, more students surrounded him. He heard snatches of what they said to him. But he couldn't make sense of it all until later.

"Yvette told me what you did for her . . . ," one face told him.

"You saved Dom, and he's my brother . . . ," another face said.

"Do you remember the time you told me I wasn't fat? That I was really pretty," a girl reminded him.

"You saved my life, man. You're the best . . . ," someone said to him.

Ernesto slowly broke away from the crowd. The girl with the amazing violet eyes was running toward him. Ernesto opened his arms, and she pressed her face against his chest, crying. She was smiling and crying, all at same time.

During those moments they embraced, Ernesto had time to reflect. He stared over the heads of the students leaving the building. They had ignored the lies that Clay Aguirre had spread. They believed him, not Clay.

Paul Morales had believed in his friend, not what Ernesto had seen.

Ernesto and Abel Ruiz had placed their faith in Paul and in Paul's belief in Cruz.

It was like what Mom's book was about. Sometimes things aren't how they look—dogs, people, situations.

Sometimes you just have to take a leap of faith.